To Stephanie Mayfield

Stuart Abrams

God Bless you!!

The Rose from Sharon

By

Stuart Abrams

1663 LIBERTY DRIVE, SUITE 200
BLOOMINGTON, INDIANA 47403
(800) 839-8640
WWW.AUTHORHOUSE.COM

This book is a work of fiction. People, places, events, and situations are the product of the author's imagination. Any resemblance to actual persons, living or dead, or historical events, is purely coincidental.

© 2003, 2005 Stuart Abrams. All Rights Reserved.

No part of this book may be reproduced, stored in a retrieval system, or transmitted by any means without the written permission of the author.

First published by AuthorHouse 08/01/05

ISBN: 1-4208-4659-0 (sc)

Printed in the United States of America
Bloomington, Indiana

This book is printed on acid-free paper.

Chapter 1

And as they discussed the dissertation of life's journeys, there was no way that the tears could not help but fall from their eyes. It was as if some eternal flame had been awakened that had been lying dormant after that incident. For awhile, no one seemed able to get through to her. It was something that was unquestionably precious to her -- a thing that was taken away from her most familiar past. But it had not been erased from the annals of eternity.

Somehow, it made an appearance that plainly seemed as if the heavens had chosen to shut its gates without listening to another soul's petition. They felt compelled to think that not another prayer needed to be prayed. Wise counsel needed to be sought, but no one knew into which corner to look.

Time had discouraged him to the point to where trying to lift himself out of the muck and mire had him spent. It was more labor than the soul could withstand. He simply dropped into an abyss more harrowing than that fiery cave. He looked at a few options that might help him see the God-given side of his known abilities. Still, a crucible had been established long before he grew fully aware of its outcomes and consequences.

If only he could touch the ground that made his forefathers see heaven's grace, in spite of the iron that was heaved upon their backs, he could then know that a new day's dawn did, in fact, exist.

"Can't nobody make me see the light. I will see it when I'm ready to see it and no time sooner!" he said. He had come to the conclusion that feeling down and out was the norm in a life, until divinity came in and made its mark. The him was Jesse Johnson. The her, Rose Johnson. The year, 1971. She was a freshman. He was a junior and a star sprinter on the track team.

Her father, the Deacon Rufus Johnson, was strict on her, but made allowances for himself. He saw how quickly his little girl had blossomed. Undoubtedly, he had determined within his own heart to guard her innocence. He used the power that the good Lord had bestowed upon his six-foot-two, two hundred and thirty-one pound frame. He was given a particular strength, even at fifty-three.

Rose would talk for hours on the phone, until her mother's voice would request to "cut it short now." She was attractive, bearing a strong resemblance to her mother, Della. They both possessed a light pecan complexion, with eyes the color of rich sable, hair the color of mocha brown. It had a fine, soft texture and they both wore it past their shoulders. Rose's musical pleasure was Diana Ross and the Supremes (the early years), Smokey, Gladys Knight, The Stylistics, The Delphonics, and The Carpenters. The Carpenters?

She'd sit in the solitude of her room with the door closed on Saturday afternoons and listen to the Carpenters' *Close to You*. She loved the verse that stated,

On the day that you were born, the angels got together and decided to create a dream come true. So they sprinkled moondust in your hair of gold, sunlight in your eyes of blue.

The song went on further, glorifying the duty of this fictional demi-god. The song would make one think of their own high school sweetheart and the elusiveness of a love everlasting. So often when she would play that song, she would lie in her bed, with its pink cotton covers, and think of the saddest song that she could sing at the hint of a whisper. While lying there, she would cry herself to sleep on the strength of self-appointed sympathy.

While lying there, she would figure out her algebra, be intrigued by Shakespeare and become engrossed in sociology. Yet she would always get distracted when she heard the tremendous roar of the trains as they went by. This distraction was a constant, whether it was in the evening, morning or late at night. The sound would become unbearable after the incident.

The Rose from Sharon

It happened on a Sunday afternoon right after church. Her friend, Angela Townsend, kept telling her that she was going to run away from home because she couldn't take the beatings from her father anymore. The welts on her legs from the beatings caused her great embarrassment.

"I can't take no more of it, Rose. I just can't take another beating from my dad," she said. Her father had already informed her that he was going to spank her after she got home from church for getting a C on a math test on Tuesday. The greater punishment her father inflicted on her was making her wait for the beatings. The mental torture far outweighed the physical.

That Sunday, she wore a white dress to church. Her brown legs were oiled up just enough with Vaseline. Her shoes were a patent vinyl with a buckle across the front. The entire congregation was bewildered when she went forward and asked for forgiveness for all that she had done. What all could she had done at the age of twelve? God had already forgiven her for the M & M's that she had slipped into her coat pocket when Mr. Kinzel, owner of Kinzel's Market went to the back to restock milk. When she hit her sister and lied to her mother about it, God had also long forgiven her. What then was the future sin unseen, except through the eyes of an omnipotent God?

There were few dry eyes after her confession. She then kissed and hugged the pastor and her friends. She also hugged Mrs. Lyons, the Sunday school teacher she felt so much fondness for. They were all exuberant that whatever had burdened her was now lifted.

When she left the church, tears flooded Angela's eyes. She loved to watch the trains. Four miles down the track, she saw a train approaching. The sun glistened on the rails like the sheen of Christmas ornaments. She smiled as she tried to perceive how much power it took to pull the massive land barges across slender slabs of steel. Something pulled her closer as her tears fell uncontrollably. The conductor kept blowing the horn as the train dragged her body for a mile-and-a-half. Her dress was turned to rags. The conductor was so shaken, he couldn't work for a week. Rose had to be medicated in order to get through her friend's funeral.

Although three years had elapsed since that Sunday afternoon, the agony made it seem as if only hours had passed. But things affected her this way. Rose was a delicate spirit whose strength came from enfolding her own love around those who were in her circumference. Her glory came in giving. Her upbringing planted the seeds of the Savior within.

But there were those rare moments when she felt the need to go back in time to a more perfect age of innocence, a period swathed in the luxury of knowing all was well. She embarked to that kingdom of the age of seven, a time when she knew the excitement of playing with Slinkies and Barbies. She felt a sense of protection.

In that time she received letters from her brother, Larry, in Vietnam. Larry was nine years older and worlds apart in enlightenment. He didn't write her about the ugliness -- the mutilation, murder and rape. Yet, she sometimes overheard her parents talk with anxious worry about it. Her big brother's words were of encouragement: stay in school, study hard, watch out for the boys, listen to Mom and Dad and "never, never forget to pray for me every night."

Rose longed for the day when she would see her brother walk through the front door again. Not just to walk in, but to be unscathed, coming in from that season of Hell. Her love for her brother was deep and unchallenged and she spoke of him as if in reverence.

Rose and her family resided in a small, predominantly black area of Sharon, Pennsylvania called Ferrell. There was little opportunity and few chances for success. In spite of how it appeared, Rose remained hopeful. There were times when she felt guilty about her feelings of hope while her brother was caught up in a winless war with no victor: Vietnam.

Rose recalled the one time her brother dared to be explicit about the war, the time when he was forced into a conflict that led to him receiving the Medal of Bravery. Upon recollection, it was a muggy Saturday morning in Saigon in the middle of the monsoon season. His platoon was on early patrol. They were more aware than what they wanted to be that death could come at any time.

All around them, in every direction, was emerald-green foliage. Its dampness bathed their boots until it soaked through the inside. It caused their socks to discolor and their feet to ache. It had been two hours of coursing through the hell of the jungle when it happened.

Suddenly, out of nowhere, a searing gun shot blasted through the stillness of the morning air. A single round penetrated the neck of Sergeant Corwin, severing his jugular and killing him instantly. The platoon was stunned. Their sweat mixed with their tears. Larry was momentarily startled. He was the only one able to zero in on the position of the sniper. Larry was the closest to the sergeant. His machine gun rang out instantly killing four enemy soldiers. He led a passageway to safety. The only sounds were the sighs of relief and the gnashing of teeth that the platoon once again escaped the hands of death. Rose's knowledge of her brother's constant threat of death hung over her. There were times that it made her edgy, uncomfortable.

Her other worry was the strictness of her father. She never did anything to give him reason for doubt. For that reason, its origin was perplexing. His concerns were unfounded for she was not like her contemporaries. She observed them and then purposed in herself to not be like those other girls who had pastors, bishops and elders as fathers. These men held their daughters in such a position of lockstep that rebellion was inevitable.

Many of the girls were in such urgency for escape that they tore their stockings climbing out of bedroom windows, in order to meet their boyfriends. They were so bold that they would dare their brothers and sisters to tell on them when they snuck out. There were those moments when Rose was unsure of the faithfulness of some of the church's representatives. On too many occasions, she would catch her father's fellow deacons gazing lustfully at the smoothness of her youthful legs. In spite of it all, she loved the church and what it represented.

During Sunday services, Rose's soul grew joyful at the preacher's words. She loved the rhythm, the rhyming, his timing, a certain pitch that he had when he said, "I love the Lord. He heard my cry and pitied my every groan. As long as I live and trouble rise, I'll hasten to His throne."

She loved the way he would lift his left leg like a drum major whenever he got excited, enthralling her. Pastor had a way, an art, at getting the crowd worked into frenzy. The voices of the choir moved her as well. The voices were Mississippi- and deep-Alabama bred.

There were deep-fried, fat-back sisters with the music of angels that they would pull up through the strength of their heavy breasts, topping their runover shoes. Their thick thighs rubbed a Holy Ghost fire of immeasurable fury.

"The Pastor preached good today and the choir really sang," Rose's mother, Della, said.

"Yes Ma'am, they did," Rose agreed.

But there were times when Della's tone was somber when the subject of the preacher came up. Her tone would drop like the temperature on a frigid January night. Della's mind reluctantly went back almost 25 years. She remembered when her uncle, Pastor Josiah Peterson, lost everythihng except his soul. In eastern Mississippi, a black man's truth was always mistaken for lies and deceit. It was a distortion born out of the preference of skin color and the paranoia of the majority power. They thought the blacker, the more deceitful; the blacker, the higher the flame of the rage; the blacker, the more the wickedness would abound.

It was June and the weather was brilliant. The sun quickly turned gold as it disappeared into the west. Darkness was on its way.

Sophia James was deadly intent on taking a stroll down the quiet streets, amid the green landscapes. Sophia's beauty was such that it would sometimes stop common strangers. Her lily-white complexion was flawless. Her eyes were the color of blue topaz. Her hair was more blond than auburn and always well coifed.

In spite of it all, she hated her whiteness. She found difficulty in accepting the lie, the abomination that said her whiteness made her superior to all other human creation.

"Momma, why am I so pale? I can't stand it," she said while wiping away tears.

"Girl, why do you talk crazy? You are a blessed child to have such beautiful skin. Don't you know you are closer to God when you're white, because after all, God is white," her mother would say in her vaunted Southern Belle manner. Sophia disdained her mother's lies and deceit, as much as she did looking at her mother's coffee-stained teeth.

"Oh really, Momma? Well how do you know that God is white since you've never seen him?"

"Why come on, girl, everyone who's got a little bit of a common sense knows that. After all, white stands for good and black stands for evil. Don't you know that?" she said, her eyes bulging in aggravation.

"No Ma'am, I didn't know that, but I guess I do now, huh?"

"Sophia, God and the angels are white and the devil is black and you know that those two don't mix. God doesn't want white folks and black folks to mix." Her mother smiled while speaking, fully convinced of her words.

"All right, Momma, if you say so," Sophia said with a sense of reluctance. She'd voice any agreement that would bring silence to her mother's lies. She was taught that blacks were mere beasts. They were beasts far less than human, savage in thinking, word, and deed. Enough had been spoken about them that she should avoid them at all costs. It only provoked her curiosity.

The sermons in the white church that she attended stated that she should never date, kiss, touch, or much less be found in the bed of a black man. Furthermore, if she were to ever give in to her base passions, she would be an outcast, nothing less than banished from her circle of family and friends. It would be cultural mutiny. It would be betrayal in its purest form. Her kindred would completely disown her.

But when she first saw Ezekiel (Zeke) Peterson, Josiah's only son, her life would never be the same. Never before had she been so captivated by a man. His skin was the color of midnight. There was a rawness, a definition to his muscles; his frame, a description out of Michaelangelo's most perfect dream. He even had perfect vein structure. They crisscrossed his arms like blades of grass in a field. His teeth were small, pearly and gleaming.

When Zeke saw Sophia, he didn't make eye contact. But she spoke anyway. She cornered him, asked his name, his address, his age.

"I'll be seein' you around, Zeke."

A week passed since their initial meeting. One night, Sophia carefully and quietly snuck out. She rapped on his bedroom window. She waited and waited for a response.

"Hey Zeke, wake up. Wake up!" she said, soft, yet forcefully, in her deep southern drawl. Zeke came out from underneath the covers in a frantic fashion.

"Girl, what is wrong wit' ya'? Ya' needs to be quiet 'fo you wake up ma' folks."

"Why don't you come out here and see me?" Sophia questioned.

"I can't. You needs ta' get on away from here befo' you get us both in some trouble," he replied.

"Come on, Zeke. If you don't come out, I'll scream."

"I can't. Don't make me do this!" he cried with a desperate plea was in his voice. Sophia's shoulder-length hair was uncombed. Her blue eyes were intense, almost sinister. At a closer view, here irises had widened to their fullest point. Zeke finally climbed out of the window, not wanting to chance the potential that she might scream. His heart raced. His genitals were in heat.

"Why don't you just leave, Sophia, befo' you gets me in a lotta trouble. Please." She grabbed his hands, both with affection and to calm him.

"Listen, Zeke, you know I like you. I like your hands, your face, your dark skin. I bet I would like..." she stopped in mid-sentence.

"But you's don't even know me. I'm beggin' you to please leave!"

"I know enough," she said.

"No ya' don't," he said.

"Lay down in the grass by this tree with me and just relax. I just wanna be close, that's all."

"Please go. Please."

"I ain't goin' nowhere 'til you kiss me."

He pecked her lightly on the left cheek wanting to do anything to suppress her potential scream.

"I wanna kiss on the mouth."

"Keep your voice down," he said.

"Don't worry 'bout it. What they gonna do to me? I'm a white girl. You'll be the one in trouble," she said with a giggle, as a fury rose in her eyes. Her words hung in the air like a nauseating funk, touching the nerve endings in Zeke's brain. His temple pulsed, his stomach grew irritated. Yet, his eyes were able to pierce through the steel in her blue eyes. He couldn't believe her callous ignorance. He saw in her a picture of death.

Sophia grabbed at his trousers, trying to loosen them. She was unrelenting but he tried to get her to let him go. She tried even harder. He fought with all that he had. She tempted him with her breasts, offered money, a new ring. He refused to weaken.

"Come on now, don't you want some of this good, white stuff?" He remained unmoved. After her prodding reached its full level, she quickly left. Her humiliation remained.

"Alright, Zeke, have it yo' way."

****

They slammed the doors open. The choir went silent. On that Sunday morning, Sophia's father, Jack James, with a group of other men, stormed into Josiah's church during Sunday morning services. They came in with mud caked on the bottom and sides of their boots and brogans. Some came in with chewing tobacco still in their jaws. Many of them were unshaven, with hats still on their heads. In their dirt-stained, heavily callused hands were rifles, cleaned, cocked and ready to fire. They wanted payment in blood for the rape of Sophia James.

"Sir, what on earth do you mean my son raped your daughter?" Josiah asked. He stood 5'10", with dark brown skin, medium brown eyes, hair salted with gray. He had a medium build, thin mustache and thick, arched eyebrows. His congregation was shocked and speechless.

"It's just what I said, preacher, and I plans on takin' care of it myself," Jack James said. The congregation prayed as their hands sweated nervously. Jack James's 6'4" frame towered and his presence enveloped the entire sanctuary.

"Now turn the boy over to us or else the whole church burns to the ground."

Josiah boldly said, "I'm gonna ask you men to leave now, unless you want to stay and worship with us, because this is the Lawd's house."

Zeke trembled. He couldn't believe what was happening. He

knew that he had done nothing. The strain on his father caused torture within. Yet, he felt free from guilt. Finally, he stood up.

"I'm right here, sa'. But I nevva hurt or raped your daughta. Not in any way."

"Boy, you callin' my Sophia a liar?" The mob went after Zeke. As they came, he never ran or even flinched. Josiah stepped in front of them before they reached Zeke.

"I can't let y'all take ma' boy. I just can't do that." His eyes stared right through the soul of Jack James. He stood there unmoved.

"How 'bout we just take you then?" Jack glared. Two men went up on the rostrum, both grabbing an arm apiece. Josiah was led out the front door of the church into a blinding midday sun, the barrels of the rifles pressed against the small of his back.

"Any of you coons try anything smart, we gonna fill ya' fulla lead," one in the group said. Josiah had no fear of what they would do to him. He'd seen death. It had knocked on his door before. He saw the byproducts of a lynching. He didn't even ask where he was being led.

"We just gonna even the score, nigga. That's all." They led him out at least two miles from that country church. Deeper still they went into the pine trees that stood tall and serene. They finally stopped in a clearing that was surrounded by pine trees. They forced him to kneel. As he kneeled, the grass stained his black robe. His underarms grew damp. His forehead was beaded with sweat.

The congregation stood by praying, speaking in tongues, calling out to the Lord for mercy, raising their hands in praise. They were fully persuaded of His goodness in spite of how things appeared.

Jack James hollered to the congregation, "I don't want y'all to ever forget what y'all saw today." He then cocked his rifle and aimed it at the back of Josiah's head. He fired a single round. The sound echoed through the tall, stately pine trees like the howling of wolves. The members of the congregation wept and tore at the ground. Feelings of abandonment rushed over them like a river gone mad. Josiah's dead body lay amidst the pines. His blood darkened the grass.

The pain never left Della. It was as real as it was when she had first heard about it.

Chapter 2

In addition to music, Rose enjoyed writing short stories and poetry. She had excellent ability in juxtaposing and coordinating sentence structure. She offered great promise in her writing.

Her teacher asked her if she would be interested in writing about sports for the school newspaper. The young man who had been doing it had resigned. Others who were asked declined.

"I don't know that much about sports, Mr. Wilson, but it sounds like it might be fun."

"Rose, you have talent, so I think this would be a good opportunity for other people to see how good you are," he said.

"Why thank you, Mr. Wilson. I'll try to do my best."

"There will be a meeting next Monday in Room 347 to discuss some things that we want to do. I'm looking forward to seeing you there, Rose."

"I'll be there."

Rose immediately began to study and to familiarize herself with the sports section. She practiced her writing style, euphemisms, and rhetoric. She read the UPI and AP wire stories.

The writers she studied were awe-inspiring. They wrote about Hank Aaron's homeruns, Walt Frazier's jump shots. They wrote of Jerry West, Gayle Sayers, and Jack Nicklaus. They sensationalized Mantle, immortalized Ali and demonized Namath. With the arrival of spring close at hand, the question now was, who would win the pennant?

"Hey Dad, who you think will win the pennant this year?" Rose asked.

"Since when did you get interested in the pennant race?"

"I'm gonna start writin' for the school newspaper, the sports section."

"What?! You don't know that much about sports. Why do you wanna do somethin' like that? They couldn't find no boys to do that?"

"No sir, they couldn't find no boys. I'll be the first girl to report sports in our school. That inspires me." A humble countenance came over Rufus.

"That's good, Rose. I'm proud of ya'. But, why couldn't they find some boy to do that?"

"Dad, I really don't know, but I feel I can do just as well as any boy."

"I'm glad you believe in yourself. I'm gonna go back to your main question though about the pennant. I think the Oakland A's with Vida Blue have a good chance. The Pittsburgh Pirates are good. I love to see the Milwaukee Brewers, with my boy Hank Aaron, but I don't know about their defense."

He stretched out his legs and let out a sigh, as he sat stoically on the sofa. He raised up and pushed back the curtains to see how the weather was. As it turned out, the sky was turning to a charcoal-colored overcast. His eyebrows raised. "It looks like rain might be coming," he said.

That Saturday morning, the rain came down with a cruel vengeance. Rose and her mother were going to Youngstown, Ohio to get an early start on shopping for Easter dresses with the holiday being only a little less than a month away. Her mother drove the blue Pontiac Catalina with caution.

Rose noticed a team of young teenage boys, black and white, jogging on the side of the road in navy blue and gray sweats. Rose admired their stride, their formation. She studied their determination, their unwillingness to relent, in spite of the constant throbbing in their abdomens.

She watched the sweat that fell from the tips of their noses, blending perfectly with the drops of the rain. Precipitation moistened the rose petals that had not yet found their way to full bloom.

"Hey Momma, look! Them boys are really getting it," she said.

"Yeah they are." Della noticed the emphasis in Rose's voice. Her tone took on a higher level.

"That's the school's track team, Mom. I recognize some of 'em."

"Calm down. You all excited and you ain't even wrote your first sports story."

"I know it's gonna be exciting though, Mom." she said.

Like a knawing wind, the harrowing voice of intrigue blew through her mind. A thick stream of blue heat and raw exuberance shot through her with the same powered trajectory of a .357.

"You need to be thinkin' about what kinda dress you gonna wear to church Easter Sunday." They arrived at J.C. Penney's. Five dresses were tried on, yet none of them held the appeal that Rose was looking for.

"You workin' my patience, girl. You need to find somethin' to wear." They walked through the parking lot to the car. On the way, Rose ran into a classmate, Jackie Cox. Jackie was a fair-skinned, stout young lady, with sad eyes and dry, unkempt hair, but with a remarkable, quick smile.

"How you doin', Rose, and how are you, Mrs. Johnson?" she asked.

"They both responded, "Fine."

"I heard you gonna be writin' for the school newspaper. I think that's really nice."

"Thanks. How'd you find that out?"

"Girl, you know it ain't hard to find out anything at that school. I mean, it's good because there ain't hardly any black kids working on the school paper, so I'm glad you agreed to do it."

"Thanks."

"How's your mother doin', Jackie?" Della asked.

"She's fine."

"Good. Well, I guess we better get goin', Rose. Jackie, tell the family we said hi."

"I will. See you Monday, Rose."

"Alright, see ya'."

Jackie's family had certainly seen better days. Her father's auto accident two years earlier had left him with both knees crushed and permanently useless. Jackie shared a twin bed with her twelve-year-old sister who still wet the bed. The bed-wetting began when she witnessed the electrocution of her best friend from a bolt of lightning while they played and did headstands three years before on the football field. Her two younger brothers shared a twin bed across the room.

"That girl really has a good outlook on life in spite of what her family's been through," Della said.

"Yes she does. She's strong."

On the trip back to Sharon, the raindrops had an uneven rhythm. Rose watched them as they glistened on the windshield. She gently crossed her legs as she looked at them. When the voice of Marvin Gaye came across the radio, the song, *Mercy, Mercy, Me* silhouetted her mind with sound. A gentleness in the voice carried the power of strumming guitars, the background voices like that of angels while Marvin questioned, *Where did all the blue skies go? Poison in the wind that blows from the north, south and east. Oh mercy, mercy me. Things ain't what they used to be.*

Della asked, "Girl, what you thinkin' 'bout? You awfully quiet over there."

"Nothing really, Momma. Just thinkin'."

When they approached Sharon, Della's foot lightened on the accelerator. She remembered that she needed to stop at the grocery store. "Your dad wanted some pigs feet."

"All right, Ma'am."

When they arrived at the house, Rose couldn't wait to get to her room and get lots in the music. The Stylistics lured her into a feeling she was trying to deny. As she listened, it all swept through her mind in the way wind devastates the silence in a valley.

You are everything and everything is you. Oh, oh you are everything and everything is you.

"Turn it down a little bit," her father called out.

Monday arrived with a stream of heaviness. Rose welcomed its appearance. Gloomy weather helped her to concentrate.

The bell that signaled the end of the school day finally rang.

The Rose from Sharon

Rose ran upstairs swiftly to the school newspaper meeting. A familiar face met her on the stairway. Everyone called him Slable, but his real name was Kevin Jackson. He was a tall, slightly built young man of seventeen, but was still in the freshman class. His lips were thick, his musculature raw. When he spoke to her in his raspy baritone, his teeth gleamed. They were as white as her father's neatly starched Sunday dress shirts.

Rose studied his eyes. She couldn't help but notice how glassy they were. Then, with the fervor of a Baptist preacher, he hollered, "Hey, Rose!"

"How you doin', Slable?" she said.

"Just mellow, baby. Just mellow," he said, his voice fading.

He moved past her, descending down the cold steps like a wise old snake, the kind that knows its territory too well. Rose then suddenly heard him say, "umh." She turned around swiftly and saw him slump against the beige wall like a soldier with a shoulder wound. He seemed weary, unable to speak nor even whisper for help. He then went to the floor. Rose screamed out his name frantically, "Slable, Slable! What's wrong, Slable? Get up!"

She could hear that his breathing was unnatural, heavier than normal, exasperated. She saw a disturbing sense of fright come over him, like one frightened by the fluorescent eyes of a cat during the cruel darkness of midnight. A trail of spittle ran down the side of his face. His legs began to buck wildly as he uttered unintelligible sounds. His breathing was violent. Rose took off to find help. She hollered down the hallway, "Help somebody, help!"

Rose ran to the nearest room to find a teacher. Mr. Lindsey, a Social Studies teacher, craned his neck out of his classroom, then ran to assist. Slable tried to holler out, but it was indistinguishable. Mr. Lindsey's efforts were to no avail. Slable had already swallowed his tongue. He lay dead with his eyes wide open.

Rose was frantic beyond belief. She felt sorry for him. She cried in agony for his soul. She remembered Slabel's sweetness, generosity and concern. She recalled the time that Susan Brown, who was much bigger and tougher, had pushed her. It was raining that day. Susan, big-boned, wide-hipped and angry, attempted to push Rose into a mud puddle. Slable walked by after smoking marijuana with his friends. He immediately intervened. Susan froze when she saw Slable.

"Leave her alone, Susan, before you have to deal with me." Susan never confronted Rose again. Rose never knew what to make of Slable. He was smooth-talking, possessed with the speed of a cheetah and the strength of a lion. Now he lay dead in the wake of his own future.

Slable was always in fierce pursuit for trying to be first. He was a father at fifteen, the first in the neighborhood to try marijuana, the first to admit to having oral six with a girl, the first to try heroin. Now he was the first to die from an overdose of its poison. Rose watched as they put a sheet over his face. She felt isolated and cold, like a child locked out from a shelter in the midst of a tortuous rainstorm.

Slable died on a Monday, but the funeral home held his body until that Saturday, the day of the funeral. This was done in order to give his relatives from Mississippi time to get to Sharon for the funeral. His family also had to give their church time to raise enough money in order to at least open the grave. The remaining payments would have to be made in installments. There was no life insurance. Slable's mother was beside herself at the funeral. She fainted twice. Her husky, 5' 3", 240-pound body was immersed in sorrow. The rest of the family was also devastated.

Slable was laid to rest in a forest green, thick-lapeled velour jacket and a mint green, ruffled shirt (the kind favored on bridegroom mannequins and prom night candidates). In addition, he wore dark green bow tie, wide enough to fit on the front grille of a Chevrolet.

****

Monday once again arrived. Rose was anxious to bury her pain in writing. On that March morning, a tumultuous wind brought under its wings a barrage that pounded the concrete with insatiable anger. It was not like the beautiful rhythm of African drums at midnight. Nothing was bold enough to steal its power.

She tried to focus, but the events of the past week kept reeling in her mind. After one of her classes, she heard pushing and shoving in the hallway. The crowd hollered, "Kick his ass, Jesse. Get him, Jesse."

The Rose from Sharon

It was Jesse Johnson, the number one man on the track team. He had just slammed Steve Caston, who had been antagonizing him for some time. It took the strength of Mr. Buxton, an English teacher and part-time weightlifter and Mr. James, a counselor and former basketball standout, to pry the two boys apart. They were marched to the office. The only thing Rose caught was a glimpse of Jesse's back.

Their punushiment was two weeks of suspension. The principal didn't even flinch as he denied Jesse the privilege of working out witgh the track team. Jesse would not be deterred and worked out on his own. He became more determined than ever. He rose early to do additional windsprints. Up and down his block, he ran with savage strength and uncanny speed. Stretching his legs like a cheetah, he took off, stopping on a dime, turning back for more punishment that would in time turn his body into a diamond. Jesse was determined to make his body into such a machine that he would win every race. He didn't want just victory, but wanted to leave his competitors arm's lengths behind.

Rose couldn't stop thinking of him. She saw him running while she walked home. His skin would glisten with sweat. She noticed how his powerful arms pumped and pushed against the wind like the wheels on a train. He ran as if trying to flush the anger from his soul so that he could find rest. His anger added dimension to his mystery. He possessed an adolescent passion at war with itself, reeling, with no captain to chart its course.

Chapter 3

After much adolescent daydreaming, Rose saw Jesse again. This time it was in a dream with brilliant colors and unusual clarity. The day had an aquamarine sky, a tangerine sun and foliage rich in 14 omnipresent shades of green – sea green, forest green, medium olive and all colors in between. The temperature was like the Mediterranean. The location resembled that of one of the Balearic Islands in Spain. This particular island that they were on was abundant with grapes, olives and citrus fruit.

It was no romantic outing, but was a life or death situation. Jesse was in the race of his life. His God-given talents needed to be as sharp as they ever were. The track that he was going to run on was enormous, the crowd immense. He was competing against the greatest athletes in the world. All of the athletes were black men from different parts of every continent. They were from Zimbabwe, Jamaica, New Guinea, Nigeria, Cuba, South Africa, Egypt, Morocco, Liberia, Libya, Australia, New Zealand, South America, pockets of Europe, and North America.

Their task was to run the 800-meter dash in a time set by the judges. The judges were all white men of British, German, Polish and French descent. They had all agreed on a time in which, if anyone failed to meet it, would die by decapitation. As the dream continued under the thunderous roar of the crowd, the runners took their respective places in the blocks. Their muscles were stretched tight under skin of brown, mocha, caramel, black, blue black and tan. While they settled into their blocks, the noise of the crows slowly subsided into a complete hush.

Nervousness charged through their bodies like good electricity gone bad. A light, tropical wind took over the stadium. Then, like a blast of pure octane fuel, they shot out of their blocks with unforgiving speed. As the elements of the air and the muscles within the flesh fought against one another, the crowd began to cheer. Sweat began to pour from them as they turned the first corner. Out of the pack, Jesse had paced himself at a solid twenty. Within seconds, he moved up to fifteen. A Nigerian speedster tried to knock him off stride, but he kept his composure. Seven more seconds elapsed and he surged to twelfth place. When Michael Draper, from Queens, New York, looked over his shoulder, Jesse stole eighth place from him. Drake Marshall from St. Louis tried to give him a shove, but he took his third place position. He then eyed the finish line as he felt numbness come into his legs. He threw his arms up in victory.

Rose continued to dream until the alarm clock rang, showing 6:05 AM on its translucent face. The voice of his mother further motivated her out of slumber.

"Good mornin', Mom," she said.

"Good mornin' to you. You act like you didn't want to let that bed go, girl."

"I got caught in this dream. It was kinda scary and kinda weird at the same time. It was about one of the boys on the track team named Jesse Johnson."

"Yeah, I saw some sports articles about him last year," Della said.

"I don't know, Mom, there just seems to be something mysterious about him." After Rose finished a breakfast of grits, sausage and scrambled eggs, she headed toward the bathroom to shower. Once she was done, she quickly went to her room and began to get dressed. She grabbed her algebra and history books and a copy of *Jane Eyre* and headed for the front door.

After a short walk, she ran into Vivian Hayes, who was also on her way to school. She was coming from the direction of the plant where Rose's father worked. They finished the distance to school together, talking about the latest spring fashions. Before they got to school, the conversation took a turn toward the subject of boys.

"So who do you think is fine, Rose?"

Unwilling to reveal her soul, Rose shied away from an answer and instead asked, "I don't know. Who do you think is cute?"

"That Ross Jenkins looks too good to be real, girl. I mean with his smooth light skin, goatee and together afro, that brother is fine!!"

"Yeah, he looks good," Rose said.

"Oh yeah, and Jesse Johnson too, girl."

"Jesse who?" Rose asked.

"Jesse Johnson! He looks good."

"Yeah, alright, but I hadn't really noticed him," Rose said as she tried nonchalantly to camouflage her lying words. "So why were you comin' from that direction, Vivian?" Rose asked.

"What direction?"

"The direction you were comin' from when I first saw you."

"Oh, that direction. I had to drop somethin' off to somebody, that's all, no big thing."

"No big thing then," Rose said. As they got closer to the school, Vivian turned several young men's heads. She had the most vivacious body in the school. She took the utmost pride in being blessed with the body of a twenty-six year-old model, although she was in fact only seventeen. Vivian had a persona to match the jazziness of her frame and a confidence that could back down the most fervent opposition.

Rose's school day went by in a blur. For the first time in some weeks, she felt as if she belonged. She did start to notice, however, that her father's behavior, for reasons unknown, was no longer what it once was. He stayed out later and left for work earlier. He was jumpy, like a child who raises his hands in defense at every move of a parent who beats him. Within a short time, raccoon-like, half-moon dark rings had formed underneath his eyes from lack of sleep. A guilt that only he was aware of was eclipsing his entire being.

Della started to notice the deep depression in his eyes. "What's wrong, Rufus? You just don't seem to be yourself these days."

"I'm alright. What makes you think somethin's wrong?" he said. A sudden throbbing started in his brain.

"Listen, I ain't no fool. I probably know you better than you know yourself," she said to him.

"Umh. So you think so, huh," he said with arrogance. Della didn't even go the level that would normally challenge her to answer him with a mind-bending comeback.

"Does this have anything to do with me, Rufus?" she asked.

"No." It was getting more and more difficult for Rose to ignore the fact that something had gone awry. She would hear others whisper but was always unable to make out what they were saying. Whenever they noticed her in their presence, they would find reason for quick dispersion. She couldn't help but feel isolated, but from what, she wasn't yet sure. She found solace in writing about the track meets. Along with her fervor for writing, she also developed an active prayer life. Her recent sufferings created a desire within her to seek those things which were of eternal consequence. She began to look for God's guidance in every manner of her life. She needed peace, now more than ever and found it through supplication with God.

One Sunday night, Rose kneeled to say her prayers after the Ed Sullivan Show. Her mind went to that morning's message. The pastor preached on salvation and it pricked her heart when he said, "The Lord can give you a song that even the angels can't sing. That is the song of salvation, a song of redemption! The angels can't sing that song because they weren't the ones redeemed. We were! They didn't sin. We did! God loved us enough to give His only begotten Son. I said, His only begotten Son!"

His voice began to resound even more as he said, "Ya'll didn't hear me! He gave His only begotten son so that we might have the right to the tree of life." His exclamations were at a fever pitch as the congregation found itself caught up in a fury.

"This was done so that we can be saved and sanctified, livin' for Him in everything that we do. This was done so that we can be a blessing. I said, be a blessing to others."

The congregation came back with a loud "Amen."

"Oh church, if you would just pray and seek God's face, He will make a difference in your life." As he concluded his message with aplomb and showmanship, thunderous applause came on like a wall of fire.

His words penetrated Rose's soul. When she descended to her knees in prayer, she prayed, "Lord, I really believe that you're real. I felt you before and I really feel your spirit with me today. Lord, you have helped me to overcome so many obstacles in my life and I am thankful for that. I am asking that you forgive me of my sins and come into my life and save me. In Jesus' name I pray. Amen."

As she climbed into bed and turned her head towards the wall, sleep fell within minutes. Rose awakened to an unfamiliar peace that she had never felt before.

"Good morning. You look like you're in a good mood this morning," Della said.

"I am in a good mood, Mom. I'm saved now. I prayed to the Lord last night and asked

Him to save me and He did. He really did, Ma."

Della then hugged her daughter tightly. "I'm so proud of you. I've prayed for this day for a long time."

That week, Rose shared her experience with her classmates and the athletes that she wrote about. Her teachers were even included in her testifying. The next Sunday, Rose woke early for prayer and meditation. She took a lukewarm shower, letting the melody of the song, *Oh Happy Day,* flow through her without effort. The streams of water cascaded down her back into the light blue porcelain tub.

Rose selected a blue dress to wear to Sunday service. As she went down the stairs, her eyes met those of her father as he sat at the dining room table. She noticed a hint of guilt in his gaze and knew something was wrong.

"Good mornin', Dad. How you doin'?"

"I'm doin' just fine, baby. How you doin'?"

"Oh, I'm doin' good, Dad." She sensed his nervous energy and said, "You say you're all right, but you look nervous."

"Whatdaya mean? You ain't getting smart are ya'?" he said.

"No sir, Daddy. I'm just concerned about you."

His eyes shot her a look of extreme suspicion. He rubbed his right thumb with his index finger, as he said, "How's the team doin' this year?"

"They're doing pretty good. Some of those boys are really fast." Della joined them at the table. When they arrived at church, they went through the ritual of speaking to everyone. Testimony time came early. Rose was the second person to speak about the goodness of the Lord.

"Giving honor to God, who is the head of my life, the pastor, pulpit members, deacons and all of God's children. I just want to stand and testify about how God has saved and sanctified me and planted my feet on solid ground."

The church walls reverberated with "Amens." She lifted her hands in praise and victory to the goodness and glory of God, who had filled her soul with His spirit. She continued for fifteen minutes. No eyes were dry. Her mother cried with joy. Her father had a thousand emotions running through him, but the most profound was guilt.

Rufus thought about when he gave his life to the Lord at the age of 16. He had such a fire for God that he even walked in and witnessed to his high school principal. Yet, at this very moment, he was fighting a battle that was pulling him between heaven and earth.

This same guilt came to visit him at night. It wrapped a vise of anguish around his neck. He stayed awake at night. His feet would become frigid as he walked the linoleum floors in his kitchen. He reached a point where he even began to think of the events in his life that formed the direction that it took. It was no mystery that most life-transforming events had momentum, a trajectory that propelled them to fruition.

His memory dragged him back 30 years to a state youth convention. It was an annual event that was established for the youth of the Baptist faith to come together to further enhance their spiritual work. More often than not, it ended up being a social event where addresses were exchanged between boys and girls. During this point in his life, Rufus had not yet figured out how to coordinate a look of distinction to attract the opposite sex. He was not nice looking, spoke well enough, and his hygiene was at an immaculate level. He couldn't understand why not one young lady ever approached him. Being a prisoner of his own shyness, he didn't approach any of them either.

What would he say? After all, his objective for going was to draw nearer to the Cross. At this juncture in his journey he didn't feel he needed to be filled with lust. But when he boarded the bus, his peers asked him if he had gotten any addresses. When he told them "no," some of them laughed.

One boy told them, "Y'all leave Rufus alone. He's the only one who came down here for the right thing. He's too smart to be comin' down here to chase after some ole girl."

The gesture was in grand style, but it couldn't save Rufus from alienation. Angst traveled through his system with warp speed. Within time, there came a return to normalcy. He continued to repeat to himself, "Someday I'm gonna show 'em that I can get the girl. Someday I'm gonna show 'em that I can get the girl. Someday I'm gonna show 'em that I can get the girl."

His determination reached an apex. Never again did he want to live in that place of defeat where he felt both helpless and powerless. Something on the inside had gone unproven and this thing ran counter to that unction of defeat that kept trying to rise up within him. He licked his lips nervously. When he arrived home, he took an examination of his soul. He went into deep research and thorough exploration. He almost immediately started up a regimen of sit-ups, push-ups, and weight-lifting. He gave up fried foods and sweets. He doubled his water intake. In time, the acne cleared up.

Those who hadn't noticed before now did. His confidence began to rise. From that time forth, he was immersed with the mission to prove a sense of identity and a need to prove his worth. The pretty girls, he wanted – the ones with pearlescent skin, hair combed ever so softly, long lashes and legs so smooth. All that it took was a thought or a slight brush with the wind for him to feel the strength of arousal come forth.

****

The Rose from Sharon

There was no certain way that he knew how to act, except with regret, after the Susan Chapman incident. She was a young lady that he dated for a brief time, who came close to dying after a botched abortion with his child. Rufus didn't talk to anyone for three days. He went on to date other girls, but the sting never left him. There were older girls that he had begun to pursue. Some of them challenged him, aided in the expansion of wisdom, and were able to nurse his ego.

In time, he found his voice. He met an upper-class girl by the name of Rose Benet. She was a young Creole from Louisiana, a woman-child with dark brown hair and fair skin like that of fine chine. She dated him out defiance, because she knew that her mother had forbidden her to date anyone who was not light-skinned. It took only two dates for her to make his head bad.

He happened to catch a glimpse through the curtains of her picture window of her kissing and hugging on a high yellow youngster named Herb Davis. It felt almost like a kick in the groin. She had led him to think that she held true affection for him. What a Shakespearean performance. Something sour and noxious went to work in his intestines. He stood still, caught up in misery for a while. He then took off in full stride to throw up all of the pain, anger, jealousy, tumult, and tragedy that had become lodged within him.

His heart had been tortured like a steel chain cutting into human flesh. All he had strength left to do was turn back toward home. In reality, had he set himself up? Whenever he met someone like Rose, he would quickly go to work on the blueprint of their future – the picket fence, the beautiful children, the respectable career, the lovely wife, with flowing hair, chiseled cheekbones and dangerous curves. She would be an exquisite cook and a lover who possessed the power to take away all pain. In spite of his failings, something in his mind would talk to him, whispering that one day redemption would be his.

****

Rose was never able to understand Vivian's smirk whenever Vivian saw her. Vivian began to wear heavier mascara, that was darker and more sinister. Her lipstick colors were now hot pink and electric red. The only drawback was that she'd also gained more weight.

In spite of all the changes that were occurring in her life, Rose was not going to let anything interrupt her writing. She was beginning to learn the members of the track team. That included the venerable Jesse Johnson who was never too far from reach.

"So what you wanna be one day, Rose, a great sportswriter or what?" he asked.

"It might not be that, but I'd like to do something that has to do with writing," she said.

"I'm sure you'd be good at whatever."

"Why thanks. I would try to do my best." Her brown eyes glistened as they reflected the afternoon sunlight.

"So what do you wanna do when you get out of school, be a great track star or somethin'?"

"I'm already that. I'd like to go to college and maybe to the Olympics and then just make a whole lot of money," he said.

"Doin' what?" she asked.

He sighed heavily. "I haven't figured that out yet."

"Well, just don't wait too late to figure out what you want to do."

"Don't worry, I won't. But, you know, when you think about running, speed is a complex thing to measure."

"What'd you mean by that?" she asked.

"I'm just saying that it means different thing to different people. It doesn't mean the same thing to everyone and everyone is not going to view it in the same fashion."

Only the two of them were left in the stadium as they sat on the hard wooden bleachers that had faded to a chalky gray. She contemplated his voice. She tried not to be taken in by his smile, but she found herself being pulled in by his words. While they sat there discussing small talk, the sun took a refuge. Gray clouds rolled in. Thunder gave warning. A bolt of lightning hit somewhere between the 30 and 40 yard line, tearing at the soil. Then the rain came with utter fury.

The Rose from Sharon

Rose and Jesse swiftly ran for cover under the bleachers until the rain subsided. In the midst of the raging storm, Rose stopped and stared deeply into Jesse's eyes without a word being passed. He quietly took her hand. He studied the tautness of her skin. He paid attention to the delicate texture of her neck, the slightness of her breasts.

"Jesse, what are you thinkin' about? It looks like your mind is going at a million miles per hour."

"Oh, not much."

"Something's on your mind."

"You know, Rose, you really are a pretty young lady." His breathing was heavier than normal.

"Why thank you, Jesse. I didn't think you noticed."

"I notice everything," he said.

"Oh, is that right?"

"Yeah, that's right. Like I noticed that it looks like you're getting chilly. You oughta let me warm you up."

"Jesse, you don't even know me like that," she said.

"Maybe not, but I do recognize that you need to be warmed up." She glanced at him with hesitation in her eyes.

"All right, just a little hug." She allowed him to take her in his arms. There was gentleness in his touch that somehow startled her. She felt safe, overwhelming comfort. And as the sweat from his warm-up sweater mingled with the fabric of her blouse, she reached up towards his face to kiss him. His eyes were startled, but unflinching.

"Where'd that come from?" he asked.

"Jesse, I don't know what made me do that."

"Naw, naw, don't apologize. I enjoyed it. Let's try it again." He grabbed her by the back of the head and put his tongue as deep down her throat as he possibly could.

"You like that?" he asked.

"It took moments for her to catch up. She took in a deep breath, as her eyes shined like new pennies. She then began to speak in a rapid pace. "Jesse, I like everything about you. I - I been watchin' you for awhile and I dig the way you look, the way you talk, the way you run, your stride. I mean, I like it all. I wonder how you feel about me."

A smile came. His eyes shifted to the rain filling in the cracks in the cement. He moved to look directly into her eyes. "That's good, Rose, real good. To be honest, I think you're really smooth too. You're cute, you're nice, you're smart. You're a good writer and a lot of people look forward to readin' what you write. I been hearin' people talkin'. It makes me feel proud to know that a beautiful young black girl is able to impress other people with her writing. I'm glad to say that I know you. I even think maybe we should go out sometime."

"You really mean that, Jesse?"

Chapter 4

"Yeah, I mean it. I wouldn't say it if I didn't mean it," he said. His words hung inside her head. She lifted her head slowly. A renewed smile took over her

"That's good to know that you speak from the heart, Jesse," she said.

"Well, in that case, maybe I can take you do dinner or a movie sometime?"

"That sounds very nice. Why don't you call me and let me know when you'd like to go?"

"I'll let you know soon. For now, the least I can do is walk you home once this weather breaks. You can dig that, can't you, baby?"

"Yeah, that sounds good to me." The rain continued. It pummeled the earth for fifteen minutes, then shifted to a rhythm they could stand. They started walking, but were blindsided by a brand-new, shiny black Buick Electra. The raindrops made it glisten even more. The interior was black leather. Inside, Rose noticed a handsome, fair-skinned young man with high cheekbones and perfect teeth. He appeared to be about the same age and happened to be smiling directly at her. She glanced at the license plates and noticed that they said Ohio.

The young man's name was Adam Townsend from Mount Hilliard, Ohio, a small community outside of Columbus. His father, a mechanical engineer with a tool and die corporation, had transferred to the Sharon plant.

Within two days, Rose saw Adam again. He was enrolled at her school and assigned to her homeroom. When he walked in the room, all of the girls' eyes fell upon him, as if he were a ten-carat diamond ring sitting in Cartier's showroom. He wore a forest green, zippered velour pullover, dark green Aztec polyester pants, green thick and thin socks, and dark-green patent leather slip-on platform shoes. He looked over and smiled at Rose and she beamed with pride. She couldn't help but notice his broad shoulders, flat abdomen and the huge muscles on the backs of his thighs. They were more pronounced in his tight pants.

Adam's eyes intentionally flirted with her like a fisherman with a large catch on his line, merely waiting for the opportune time to reel it in. They made their acquaintances and then waited for the first bell to ring.

After her third class, Jesse was waiting in the hallway in order to carry her books. "What's happenin', Rose?"

"How you doin', Jess?"

"Rose, you ain't gonna believe what Mr. Pendelton tried to do today!"

"What did he try to do?"

"He tried to suspend me."

"For what?"

"He said that I was being belligerent and disrespectful just because I told him he was wrong for making ugly remarks about blacks and slavery. I just told him I didn't like it at all.

Then, after all that, he sent me to the office and Coach Morris happened to be there. He pleaded my case so instead of suspension, I have to do three days of detention. I can still at least stay on the team," he said.

"Don't you think it's more important that you're not getting kicked outta school than it is to remain on the track team?" Rose asked.

"Yeah, that's more important, but track is important too."

Vivian then swaggered down the hall with an evil eye targeted at Rose. Her eyes were bloodshot, the lids swollen from crying. Vivian had visited the school nurse before her first class and found out that she was pregnant.

When night fell, Rose's inability to sleep was treacherous and unforgiving. Every time she fell asleep, she would find herself in the hands of a nightmare. As the morning sunlight frustratingly moved her out of bed, her linens were turned inside out from terrors of dreaming about nauseating things.

She sat at the kitchen table looking the window. She rubbed her eyes when they became sore from staring at a robin perched on the neighbor's faded backyard fence. Her mother hummed softly. Her father had once again left early for work.

"You look like you didn't get any sleep last night, but that ain't gonna stop you from getting your butt ready for school."

"I'm not gonna let it stop me from getting ready for school."

"Well, why couldn't you sleep, Rose?"

"I guess because of all these crazy dreams I kept havin'."

"I told you about eatin' pizza before you go to bed," her mother said.

"No, Momma I don't think that was it. It was more like something was wrong or something will happen," she said.

Rose made haste in finishing her light breakfast of Corn Flakes and a slice of cantaloupe. Then she bathed in a tub of warm water. Stevie Wonder's *I Was Made to Love Her* played on the radio. The warmth of the water was rejuvenating to her. Within five minutes she dozed off. As the water started to cool, she woke and emptied the water from the tub.

While drying off, her mother hollered out her name. "Rose! Rose, hurry up out the bathroom."

"What's wrong, Momma?" Della was not sure if there was any breath left inside of her.

"Rose, you need to hurry now. That was your father's job. He just experienced a heart attack and he's in the hospital in intensive care!"

"Oh my God, no!" Rose shouted.

"Momma, Momma, it's gonna be alright."

Della quickly composed herself and said, "We don't have a lot of time. We've got to get to the hospital."

Rose ascended the stairs as if in flames. She dressed in minutes and met her mother at the car. As they drove to the hospital, Rose's hands trembled. "Momma, did you call the school?"

"Yeah, Rose."

She glanced over at her mother. She noticed the tears that were falling from her mother's eyes. They angled down the contours of her mother's cheeks and dropped onto her blouse. They arrived at St. Joseph's Hospital in seven minutes, normally an eleven-minute trek from their residence. They moved swiftly through the doors and followed the sign that said "Intensive Care." They arrived at the desk where an attractive, red-haired, blue-eyed nurse sat.

"We're here to see Rufus Johnson. Can you help us?" Della asked the nurse.

"Are you his wife?" the nurse asked.

"Yes, and this is our daughter."

"All right, Ma'am, just follow me." When they entered the room and Rose saw the needles in her father's arms, she felt weak. She wasn't sure if her strength could sustain her.

"Momma, we just got to pray and be strong and God will do the rest," she said.

"I know, Rose. I know."

Her mother sat down slowly with a certain emotional caution in the unyielding plastic chair. She prayed for her husband with fervor, as if pleading for her own life. Rose felt powerless as she stared at he father with tears glazing her eyes.

Dr. Levinson, one of the top cardiologists in the area, walked in the room with a look of neutrality on his face. He walked over to Della and said, "Mrs. Johnson, I presume? My name is Dr. Levinson."

"Yes sir. Are you the one in charge of my husband?" Della asked with hysteria in her voice.

"Yes, Ma'am."

"Is he gonna be alright?"

"Well, Mrs. Johnson, this is a tough case."

"How tough?"

"Is this your daughter?" he asked while smiling at Rose.

"Yes. Her name is Rose."

"Nice to meet you Rose," he said while extending his hand. "If

The Rose from Sharon

you would excuse us, Rose, I would like to go out in the hallway and talk to your mother."

"Yes sir." An even more distraught look now overtook Della.

"Mrs. Johnson, like I said, this is a tough one. There was some muscle damage, that much I can tell, and that is irreparable. We are going to do everything we can to pull him through this."

"Thank you, doctor."

"I want to perform surgery, but I want to get him stronger before we bring him under the trauma of the knife."

"Well, Doc, I believe in prayer and I believe God can make a way out of no way," she said.

"That's good. He's gonna need it, because the next twenty-four hours are crucial."

"I'll go along with whatever it'll take to make him better," Della replied.

"So I have your verbal consent?"

"Yes."

"Good, because we're gonna do what it takes."

"Thank you, Doctor."

"Mrs. Johnson, your husband is a fighter and he's strong, so you can take comfort in the fact that he's not gonna just give up."

"Oh, I know that too well, Doctor."

"Well, let me get back to work, Ma'am."

"Thanks for the information, Doctor." Rose came out of the room and she and Della walked down the hallway towards the lounge. The forest-green, vinyl-covered chairs gave only minimal comfort. Rose found a *Reader's Digest* magazine that contained an article about the evils of abortion and the sanctity of life. Della was up out of her seat at least five times within a twenty-minute period.

"Momma, you really need to try and relax and just believe that Daddy's gonna be all right."

"I think I need to go and call your brother in Minneapolis, Rose." Della said, her hand shaking in an unstable way.

"I can try and call him myself right now for you, Momma, if you want."

"I can do it, Rose," she said.

"Alright then, Momma."

"So tell me who this girl is at school who's pregnant." Della said.

"I have no idea. I hadn't really heard anything like that."

"I think she's in the 11th or 12th grade," Della said. "I think it begins with a V, maybe Vicky, Valerie or Vivian or somethin'."

Silence came into the room. The beige-colored walls felt like prison bars.

"Naw, naw. I know it can't be her," Rose said.

"It can't be who?"

"Vivian. You know her, don't you?" Rose asked

"Vaguely."

"How did you find out, Ma?"

"Mrs. Baylor was talkin' about it a couple of days ago at the beauty salon when I went to get my hair done."

"Oh, really?"

"They said the girl's mother is about to put her out already." Within minutes a nurse with auburn colored hair was standing right in front of Della.

"Mrs. Johnson, we're sorry."

"Sorry about what?"

"It seems as if your husband has slipped into a coma."

"Oh my God! No Lord Jesus, No! This can't be happenin'." Rose began to cry, but went to hug her mother and reassure her that everything would be all right. The nurse put her hand on Della's shoulder in the spirit of reassurance.

"I'm sorry, Ma'am," the nurse said.

"Excuse me, Ma'am!" Rose hollered.

"Yes?"

"Can we at least go and see him for awhile? We won't stay long."

"Sure, that'll be fine."

When they left the room relatives from both sides of their families were out in the lounge. Della and Rose talked to them for about thirty minutes and then left.

The next morning, Rose's stomach could only handle a glass of orange juice. Her sleep had been uneven. The heaviness in her heart transferred its way into the classroom. Her eyes were bloodshot. It

The Rose from Sharon

was impossible to hide the dark rings underneath them.

"Girl, what's wrong with you?" Adam said.

"I'm tired. I didn't sleep too well last night. My father's in the hospital."

"What's wrong?"

"He had a heart attack and now he's in a coma." Adam held Rose in his arms as she cried tears into the polyester fabric of his navy-blue, cross-stitched sweater.

"He's gonna be OK though, Rose," Adam said, doing the best he could to comfort her.

When the bell rang, she said, "Thanks for the concern Adam."

"No problem. Anytime," he replied. As she walked away, he couldn't help but notice the perfectly curved symmetry of her calves. She was seven steps away from her biology class when she ran into Jesse.

"How's your Dad doin'?" he asked.

"How did you know?"

"Did you forget that you told me about it last night?"

"Oh my God, my mind is a blank, Jesse. I'm sorry."

"That's all right. I understand you're under a lot of pressure. Just remember how tough your dad is. He'll come through this."

"I wanna believe that."

"I'm here when you need me," he said.

"Thanks." Jesse then pulled out from behind him a single crimson long stemmed rose. Rose grabbed him and hugged him tightly.

"I don't even know what to say, Jesse, except thank you." She felt the Spirit speaking these words to her heart, *My child, you are made in my image and my image is both invincible and all-powerful. Therefore, there is nothing that I, the Lord, thy God cannot see you through.*

Its grip was such that goose bumps began to trail down her arms at breakneck speed. All the while her focus on biology stayed clear.

When she arrived home, her mother met her at the door. Her face was etched with concern. "Let's get to the hospital, Rose. Your father hasn't come out of his coma yet."

"Yes, Ma'am." Della's face was angled toward the west. Her sighs emptied themselves into the air.

When they returned to the hospital to visit Rufus, he had not yet returned to himself. As they stood over him, they felt helpless. They heard the sound of footsteps in the hallway that kept coming closer and closer.

"Who can that be?"

They both peeked into the hallway and Della said, "Lawd, have mercy."

Rose said, "I don't believe it." Her brother, Larry, reached out and hugged Della and then Rose.

"How you doin', boy?" Della asked.

"I'm doin all right, Momma. How you doin'?"

"I'm fine, just worried about your daddy."

"How serious is it?"

"They don't really know just yet. Right now he's in a coma," Della said.

"When did all this happen?"

"It happened at work. I don't know if your dad is under a lot of pressure. He don't like to talk about it. I know he could eat better, but he just don't wanna give up that pork. He might have to now."

"So how you been doin', Rose?" he asked.

"I'm doin' all right, big brother."

"How many boyfriends you got now?" he asked, as his mother rolled her eyes at him.

"Why you always tryin' to start somethin'?" Della said.

"I was just playin', Momma."

Larry stood 6'1" and carried the build of a heavyweight contender. His skin was medium-brown in tone, and he had a blow-out Afro and a goatee with a slight reddish tint. He wore a three-quarter length, black leather jacket with large lapels, brown polyester pants, a brown polyester shirt with paisley print, and black platform lace-up boots that were the best that Stacey Adams offered.

They all went back in to look in on Rufus.

"At least he looks peaceful, Momma. Maybe that means he's not in a lot of pain," Larry said.

"Maybe so, but the doctors can't really tell how much heart

damage your daddy had."

"That greasy food is what clogs up your arteries. That's what my biology teacher was tellin' me," Rose said.

"I should be watchin' what I eat too. I eat a lot of burgers and fries. You know, on-the-run kinda food," Larry said.

"Did you eat yet, Larry?" Della asked.

"Not really, Momma, but I'll get somethin' pretty soon."

"I got a little somethin' at the house that I made earlier, but I think Rose and me are gonna go to the hospital cafeteria. Why don't you just go with us?"

"Not a bad idea, Momma. I'll tell you what, I'm buyin'," he said.

Della noticed burn marks on Larry's right thumb and index finger. "That ain't nothin', really. I don't even remember how that got there," he said.

"Anyway, where you workin' at now?" Della asked.

"I'm selling cars, Buicks," he lied.

"So how long you been doing that?"

"Couple months at least."

"And they let you take vacation time and you ain't even been there for a year?"

"Yes, Ma'am."

"Larry, I don't believe that." Della frowned as she spoke, taken aback by his nerve.

"Why would you wanna call me a liar, Ma?"

"Because you been doin' it for so long," Rose mumbled under her breath, diverting her eyes away from him.

"Rose, why don't you mind your own business?" he shot at her. Rose simply returned to him a snicker.

"Yeah Mom, I'm even drivin' a Buick now. It's a brand new burgundy Riveria with leather interior, a sun roof, and an 8-track with FM stereo."

"That sounds really sharp, Larry," Della said. Suspicion continued to turn in her head.

"Oh Momma, it's really nice. I'll give you a ride in it while I'm here or you can drive it yourself if you want."

"Well, once Rose gets finished with her ice cream, we'll go and look in on your father," Della said. They pushed the elevator button that took them back to Rufus' room. When they arrived, they noticed two large nurses standing over his bed.

"Mrs. Johnson, we didn't know whether you had left or not," one of the nurses said. Della felt weakness come over her like the cold swoop of darkness. Larry held her by the shoulder with the palm of his left hand, as his right hand helped to guide her into the chair.

"Momma, you need to sit down and try to relax. Worryin' ain't gonna change a thing. I know you're probably full, but I'll go get you a glass of water," said Larry.

"Thank you, son," she said, feeling lightheaded.

He walked out with the nurse who had taken his father's pulse. He asked her if she would take the water back to his mother, then stepped out for fresh air. When he came to his car, he reached underneath his seat for a plastic bag. Its contents resembled dark-green dried spinach. He opened the glove box with an oval shaped end key with GM, MARK OF EXCELLENCE inscribed on both sides. He retrieved the rolling papers, carefully placed in the dark green marijuana inside and licked the paper in order to seal the joint. As he went to close the glove box, his arm accidentally bumped an object that was dangling on a string from his rear view mirror. It held for him sentimental value that most could not understand.

It was the skeletal head of a monkey with the top of its skull removed. The bone had turned a dull gray color. It represented one of the first experiences he had in Vietnam. The majority of his platoon had just survived one of its most vicious enemy attacks. The injuries were ugly and brutal.

As the evening made an effortless pilgrimage into night, a sense of celebration was in the air. Beer began to flow. Marijuana filled the air with a sophisticated funk that swaggered in the midst of the trees. Some of the platoon members were seasoned veterans and had become acquainted with some of the customs. A local delicacy that they had discovered was monkey brains. When a monkey was killed, the membranes were eaten right out of the skull after it had been smashed with a blunt object.

Memory pulled him back to the present as he sat back in his maroon leather seats. Clouds of smoke swirled around the interior as he took long drags on the joint. When the last fibers of the joint became smoke, he pulled out a bag of white powder. He then pulled out a small tray and a single-edged razor blade. As he snorted down the four lines that he prepared, the numbing effect of the cocaine oozed through his nervous system like intricate electric lines. He turned the key in the ignition, slid in an 8-track tape and listened to Sly and the Family Stone, as they sang, *I Want to Take you Higher.*

Larry reclined both his mind and his back as the drugs reverberated inside of him. The horror of Vietnam brought forth anguish, as he recalled the stench of death. The thought of youthful slaughter made his stomach wretch.

As Larry slipped deeper into darkness, his father slipped deeper into a coma. He got out of the car and closed the door with the same caution that an undertaker uses when closing a casket. Guilt had set in and soon after, he found himself asking the question, "Why do I do these things?"

When he went back into the hospital, his guilt began to overwhelm him. He felt horror for lying about the car sales position, when in fact, he was a salesman of another sort. When he entered the room, Larry offered up silent prayers for his father's recovery. The night moved in without apprehension and comfort was found in the warmth of its darkness.

Dr. Levinson arrived to make a prognosis. "If he makes it through the night, he'll be out of danger, but right now it's touch and go," he said.

"What are the odds right now, Doc?" Larry asked.

"Your dad's a strong man and that is certainly in his favor. Given that factor alone, his chances are put into a much better light. But one thing that must be kept in mind is that there was some heart damage," he cautioned. With that news, they all went home.

The night slowly slipped into its deepest sleep. Just as the night became darker, so did Rufus's condition. At 6:00 a.m., Della was awakened abruptly from sleep. It was like a jolt from God. She sat up in bed as if an invisible hand had lifted her.

In the hospital, at the same exact time, Rufus's eyes opened and he called out in a monotone voice, "Della." He called several more times with more intensity every time. His heart rate slowly regained its normal strength. His body temperature returned to normal. There was still a burning sensation on the left side of his brain. Until then it was as though a hot curling iron had been placed inside his head. His hand quivered, as he slowly turned from right to left. His eyes tried to find their focus in the white sanitary room.

Della made haste in preparing to go to the hospital. She went to Rufus's room and found him to be alert. Her joy was unspeakable. "How you feelin', baby?" she said.

"I don't know, Della, I don't know. I guess alright. I'm just glad to be here," he said.

"You and me both."

There was still a sense of uncertainty. She grabbed his hand, but took caution not to squeeze it, as he said, "I'm hangin' in there, baby."

"Don't overdo it. Don't talk too much. Just rest so you can get your strength back," she said. She went to the phone to call Larry.

"Your dad is awake," she said.

"That sounds good, Mom. I'll be there as soon as I get dressed and eat."

"See ya later, son."

Rufus felt extreme exhilaration, after having such a discourse with death. Yet, something continued to engage him with the pain of Hell.

His face lacked proper symmetry. The more Della observed him, the clearer it became. She discovered that his right eye literally sagged one-eighth of an inch down from its origin. Muscles which had held the bottom lid in place had experienced damage during the time of the coma. It had not only affected the muscles, but also the color, changing it three shades of a lighter brown. It was also replete with a sallow cast in the lower right-hand corner. There was numbness in two fingers that would come and go like the tide at midnight. He described all of this to Della. She became discouraged.

Della went home at noon to start preparing dinner for Rose and Larry. When Rose came home from school, she sensed an aura of exhilaration, such as when a child is born into a family.

"Your dad finally woke up today, Rose."

"Thank you, Jesus!" Rose shouted.

"Ain't God good?" Della asked. Her hands raised in praise and victory.

"All the time," Rose said.

"Well, after we finish eatin', I'll take you up there to see him."

"I can't wait," Rose said, chewing faster.

"Now take your time eatin'. I don't want you getting sick."

"Alright, Momma."

When they arrived, she ran to hug her father. "Daddy, I'm so glad to see you."

"I'm glad to see you, baby," he said.

"I really prayed to see this day, Daddy."

"Well the Lawd definitely heard your prayers."

"You doin' alright, Rufus?" Della asked.

"Yeah, I'm doin' alright."

"Good."

"So how's school goin', Rose?" he asked.

"Pretty good, but kinda boring sometimes."

"You've got to remember, Rose, that school, just like anything else, is just as boring as you make it out to be."

"I guess you're right."

Rose couldn't help but be distracted by the sound of cheap dress shoes clonking in the hallway. They didn't even have a rhythm to them. There was something irritating about it all. She ducked her head out the door to see just what it was. The annoying sound was made by Ricky Evans. His life would never be the same. When Rose walked up to him, he was crying and hollering as if all sense of hope had gone.

Ricky was 13 years old, bi-racial, mildly retarded and had just seen his mother die, the only one in the world who loved him. He was a big thirteen, with emptiness in his eyes and oftimes, a look that longed for someone to love him. He was as big as he was because his mother spoiled him with food high in carbohydrates, but low in nutrients. It had gotten to the point to where, when he didn't get these foods, he would throw temper tantrums. Whenever he would act out, his stepfather would inflict punishment on his mother for not giving him what he wanted.

The black and blue marks became a regular event in the

household. When Ricky was seven years old, his stepfather choked him until he vomited so violently that his mother swore that she could see chunks of his intestines. After that, his fear paralyzed him into unresponsiveness. After that, his mother said very little to his stepfather but the deed wasn't forgotten.

A few days afterwards, Ricky's stepfather became ill with what seemed to be the flu. His mother nursed him everyday with aspirin, juices and chicken soup, but he grew worse. Within three days, he was dead. While she nursed him with chicken soup, Ricky's mother was also inflicting her husband's system with small doses of poison that she gradually increased daily until it fulfilled its purpose.

Although she never had to live in fear of him again, the guilt ripped at her. She started to drink until it snowballed into something truly ugly. She was having trouble sleeping, so sleeping pills also became her friend.

A year and a half prior to her death, she was diagnosed with cirrhosis of the liver. That, along with a broken heart, was the thing that killed her. She had been ostracized from her family for years. No one cared for her, so there was not a lot of care and concern for Ricky.

Rose walked up to Ricky and asked him what was wrong.

"It's my momma, she dead."

"I'm sorry to hear that," she said as she opened her arms inviting him to hug her. His tears stained the shoulder of her blouse as he hugged her tightly.

"Ain't nobody gonna take care of me now," he said. "I'm all alone. Yes I am. Don't nobody love me. Won't nobody care for me like my momma did."

"Why do you say that?" she asked.

"Because it true."

"By the way, what is your name?" she asked.

"My name Ricky, Ricky Evans."

"Alright Ricky, my name is Rose."

"That's a pretty name," he said.

"Thank you."

"My grandma is all I got and she real old."

The Rose from Sharon

"I don't think I can take care of you Ricky, but your grandma will take good care of you."

"You ain't me. Now I ain't got nobody to make me grits and mashed potatoes and corn. I ain't got nobody to go and buy me no Hostess Ho Ho's and Twinkies like my ma did."

"I can't do all those things, I'm only fifteen, but I will be your friend if you'd like," she said.

"Would you really?"

"Yeah, you're a nice guy, Ricky." He hugged her again.

"I better get back to my father's room now."

"OK."

"Where do you live, Ricky?"

"The north side. I don't know the street name, but the number is 417. It's over by the baseball park. You know where I'm talking about?"

"Yeah. I think so. I will try and check on you soon."

"Alright," he said.

Chapter 5

Not one of his competitors laughed at his words. In fact, they were incensed. One of them had his fists balled up, ready. As he continued to talk, his words were building a dangerous passage. He navigated well in pouring salt into open wounds.

James Johnson had developed a knack for making enemies. He walked in talking big about the two thousand dollars he had in his pocket. There was no fear within him. Some of that could be attributed to his size. He was a squared-off 5'10" with broad shoulders, and well-define arms. During his younger years, he was a Golden Glove champion endowed with a deadly left hook. He had a reputation for not only defeating his opponent, but in spitefully punishing them in the process. After handing them defeat on a bloodstained, silver platter, he would trash-talk them by calling them "tramps" and "bums."

For those reasons, it was not unusual that some mysteries remained hidden. The police still had no leads or clues after all these years as to who shot him in the back of the head and dumped his body in a shallow grave two counties away. When he would think about it, the anger would take James's son, Jesse, out of his body. It would then swallow him with sorrow.

"That sorta narrows it down to a married man," Rose said.

"What do you think then, a young blood or an old skeezer?" Jesse asked.

"It's a hard one to call. It could go either way."

The Rose from Sharon

"Vivian's a wild girl. She's just out there like that," Jesse said, as he moved his chair closer to Rose, trying not to further scrape mint-green painted porch. Then with the sly move of a cat he placed his hand on Rose's soft thigh.

"If you don't get yo' hand off my leg, it's gonna be trouble, cause I'ma slap you in the name of Jesus!"

"I'm sorry, Rose. I got beside myself."

"Just don't let it happen again."

"All right."

"It's getting late and I need to be goin' now, Jess."

"I'll give you a call later then. Is that alright?" he asked.

"Yeah, that's cool." Jesse walked her to the end of the sidewalk.

The warmth of the sun caused beads of perspiration to form on both of their foreheads. It was so inviting that Rose raised her head in order to take in its mandarin rays. She looked across the street and noticed a house whose shingles were brown with dirt. The grass in the front yard was almost five inches high. It was not completely clear to her from that distance, but it was the lone figure on the porch that somehow drew her towards the house. She was in such haste to cross the street she almost didn't see the maroon Ford LTD wagon that passed right in front of her.

"What you doin', Rose?" Jesse asked as he trailed behind her.

"I'm crossin' the street. What does it look like I'm doin'?"

It was Ricky Evans on the porch. The left side of his face was swollen from running into a wall while trying to get milk from the refrigerator the night before.

"Oh my God, Ricky. I wasn't even able to make out who you were from across the street. "How'd you do that to your face?"

"I ran into a wall last night. It really hurts, Rose."

"I'm sorry, Ricky." Jesse stood there dazed and unsure. He was trying to make a correlation between these two, whose lives were polarized by their life experiences.

"Hey, Jesse," Ricky said.

"What's hap'nin', man?"

Jesse whispered in Rose's ear, "Where do you know him from?"

"The hospital."

"The hospital?" Jesse asked.

"Who's takin' care of you now, Rick?" she asked.

"My grandma."

"That's nice."

He was not being cared for by his grandmother, but simply existing in her oblivion. His grandmother, along with being old, was also senile. She'd had poor hygiene in her youth and had backslid threefold in this the winter of her life. Even more indication of this fact was the putrid odor emanating through the screen door from the house. The stench hit Rose like a jolt of hot, forced air blown into her face without warning.

She looked into Ricky's eyes and couldn't help but feel a river of sadness. A band of sympathy marched through her mind with perfect cadence. They looked at one another, then Ricky walked slowly into the house.

"See you later, Rose."

"Take care, Ricky."

"Jesse, do you ever see this so-called grandmother around anywhere?"

"Naw, but check it out. I always see him talking to the old woman next door. She seems to be concerned about him," Jesse said.

"How can you tell she's concerned?"

"You can just tell," he said. As they talked, the silky voice of Lou Rawls singing *Love is a Hurting Thing* emanated from the radio in the house next to Jesse's.

"What's the woman's name?" Rose asked.

"Eleanor Rainey, but everybody calls her Miss Suzie."

"Why they call her that?"

"Rose, I don't know. But they do say that she knows that old voodoo mess."

"There you go again, Jesse."

"No seriously, they say that if you cross her, she'll put a spell on ya'."

"Jesse, you're a trip."

Chapter 6

Two weeks passed. Rose was eventually led her to go and pay Miss Suzie a visit. As she approached Miss Suzie's street, she watched the sun's heat bring up steam from the wet concrete. It rose like translucent flames of fire. Rose felt encouraged.

When she arrived, she discovered jungle-like crabgrass in the yard. The shrubbery was out of control and was encroaching on the porch. She could see that the screen on the door had been torn and sewn back together in a cheap manner. Rose hit the doorbell, but not hearing it echo through the living room, knew that it was broken. She tried to peer inconspicuously through the screen but saw only shadows. She tried to hold her breath to avoid the putrid odor.

Eventually, a weak and hacking voice said, "Who is it?"

"My name is Rose Johnson. Ricky's friend."

"Come on in." When Rose opened the door, she found Miss Suzie sitting in a lawn chair. Rose thought it strange, seeing other furniture in the dining room. Out of wisdom, she never questioned the motive. As it came to be known, Miss Suzie hardly ever sat down. Some even said they heard her snoring while standing up.

Miss Suzie's face was mocha-colored and semi-smooth, but her lines were more pronounced since she had not yet put in her teeth. Her eyes were bloodshot and were a washed-out brown. Cigarette smoke leered from her ashtray like a cobra on the prowl. In the corner of the kitchen, two cats with light gray eyes darted out, as if in terror. They looked thin and sickly. There were two empty cans of cat food on the kitchen counter, yet the cats seemed hungry.

"Why don't you have a seat, Rose? You want something to drink? I got some good ice water in the refrigerator."

"No Ma'am."

The unpleasant odor continued to override Rose's ability to concentrate. It was so strong that Rose was almost compelled to ask about its source. The source of the problem was Miss Suzie's beloved 15-year-old beagle, Pierre. An AMC Matador was traveling 10 miles over the speed limit and was unable to stop in time. The death of her dog made a more profound effect on her than even the death of her late, drunken husband. She was not about to let death do a separation act on her and Pierre. The day that the dog was killed, a day afterwards, Miss Suzie and one of her neighbors put Pierre's body in a crate and laid it in a crawlspace underneath the house.

"So tell me how you been doin', Miss Suzie."

"Miss Suzie's doin' pretty good considerin' I'm 72, going to be 73 in a couple of months."

"Congratulations."

"Only problem is, when the weatha' gets damp, my bursitis starts to actin' up. And don't even mention when my gout start to actin' up." Miss Suzie gave a giggle as if she were trying to mask the years of pain her eyes had seen.

"So what's on yo' mind, chile?" Her voice rose in authority.

"Ricky. How's he doin'?" Rose asked.

"Lawd chile, how long you done known that boy?"

"About a month. I met him at the hospital when his mother died," she said.

"That was too bad, cause she was all that po' chile really had," Miss Suzie said.

"Yes Ma'am, I could kind of tell that by the way he was carryin' on. I mean he was completely..."

"Po boy don't really have nobody. His grandma is a lot older than me and she can't hardly do for herself, let alone him. That's why I go over and do what I can. But I can only do so much."

"Where's his dad at?" Rose asked.

There was a pause that stunned Rose. "He don't even know who his daddy is. Lawd, chile, his mamma was married to a white

The Rose from Sharon

man and he's gone. He didn't do nothing but abuse the boy anyway. Ricky's real daddy is a black man who lives right here in Sharon."

"Is that right?" Rose asked.

"Ricky's momma was in a very bad marriage. Every weekend for awhile, the police was over there because that hillbilly was beatin' her up all the time."

"So you know this man? Ricky's real father?"

"Sho' do. Ricky's mother was a strict Baptist down in West Virginia before she moved up here. She was unable to find a white Baptist church that she felt comfortable at. She began to start visiting black churches. She finally found a black church she felt comfortable in. She eventually joined. One Sunday, she met a man while visiting church. They stated talking. They became closer. After awhile, it just seemed that the meaner her husband got, the closer she got to this other man. This other man really made her feel special." Miss Suzie hesitated, got out of her chair and poured herself a glass of ice water from the refrigerator.

"I'll tell you what, Rose. That woman really tried hard to stay faithful to her husband, but he just kept on mistreatin' her. I give her credit for tryin' to make it work. You know, I really think she cared for that man. I don't think it was no accident that she got pregnant," Miss Suzie said.

"What was his name?" Rose asked.

"I don't think you need to know that," Miss Suzie replied.

"Why? I might know him." At first, apprehension shattered Miss Suzie to the point of silence. Then, as her mind shifted into a breathable speed, she decided to hold her peace. Rose sniffed out the uncertainty within Miss Suzie. She noticed her now looking away when asked certain questions. Was something being concealed? She noticed an air of hostility that she couldn't put a finger on.

"So you really don't want to talk about Ricky's father, huh?"

"No, Rose, I really don't," she said.

"I guess maybe I should go now. You have a good day, Miss Suzie."

"Yeah baby, you have a good day too." As Rose walked home, her mind became flooded with questions. Who was Ricky Evans?

****

Vivian gave birth to an eight-pound, seven-ounce boy two weeks before scheduled. Her mother and just one of her sisters came to the hospital. The others had found themselves caught up in their own world of embarrassment and illogical anger that they had turned against their sister. For two days, she agonized over a name. She settled with Vincent. The name of the father was left blank on the birth certificate.

The boy had Vivian's nose and lips but his skin tone and eyes were unmistakably his father's. His hair was short, with soft curves on the side, giving the indication of so-called "good hair." When he cried, there was enough volume and power in his voice to bring the entire city block to attention.

Two months after Vincent's birth, Rufus was strong enough to walk three blocks a day. He did not even see the child until he was six months old. When he did, it was on the steps of a drug store that Vivian was coming out of.

"Well, Deacon Johnson, ain't you going to speak to your son and me?" she asked.

"Vivian, how are you?"

"I'm doin' alright, but I want to know if you plan on doin' something for your son and me anytime soon?"

"You know I will once I get back to work and start feelin' better. Believe me, I ain't trying to turn my back on you or the kid," he said. There was a silent irritation building on the inside.

"I hear what your mouth is saying, but actions speak louder."

"Oh, I'm going to show you, trust me on that."

"Well, tell me this, Deacon, do you plan on claimin' yo' son?" At that point an acute numbness began to disturb the inner parts of his psyche.

"Why would you even want to ask me something like that? You think that I wouldn't claim it?"

"He's not an 'it,' he's your son. I don't know what to think of you," she said, her voice rising in anger, her eye twitching.

"Well, you can just believe that I'm going to do the right thing."

"Well, since you want to do the right thing, how about letting me have $20?"

"Now you know I been outta work for months. What makes you think I got any extra money to give you when I'm barely makin' it myself?"

"Oh, so you call givin' to your son extra money? I ain't askin' you for extra money. This is money that I need. This is out of necessity that I even asked you for it."

"Right, right," he said.

"This is your child too, Rufus. You should be trying to do whatever you can for no other reason than that," she said, while pointing her right index finger five inches from his nose.

"Right, right," he repeated. But he said it in a spirit of compliance that led her to believe that all that he wanted to do was diffuse her fury.

"I only want what's right and I intend on getting it one way or another. You can believe that!" Her words came at him so sharply that it made him dizzy.

Chapter 7

He looked down at his dark-brown patent leather Flagg brother's platforms with the brown velour piping on the side. Rufus felt like a volcano was erupting violently in his brain. He rubbed his forehead in agony, as a huge vein appeared on the left side of his temple. What could he do?

He strived to make sense of his emotions, but fell short. He loved his wife, but something kept drawing him to Vivian. Could he keep this lie from Della?

Rufus walked home with the universe on his shoulders. Della met him before he reached the door. She had a look sadness which he had not seen in some time. He likened the look to a child who had lost hope in a parent. Her eyes were puffy and shiny like marbles.

"Rufus, your Uncle Charles in Alabama just died sometime last night," she said.

"Oh, no," he said. His heart sank quickly. "What was wrong? What happened? I mean, he wasn't even sick," he said. As he moved, a surge of electricity took over.

"He wasn't really sick, Rufus."

"Well then, what went wrong?" he asked.

"He had a heart attack, Rufus. His heart stopped."

Rufus took a deep breath and raised his head to the sky. The view of the beige ceiling seemed for the moment, comforting. His eye became transfixed on a Crisco oil stain on the ceiling that came from frying chicken. He again took in a deep breath and exhaled

The Rose from Sharon

intently. He wrung his hands in frustration.

"How's everyone else holding up?"

"They're as good as can be expected, I guess, Rufus. But are you all right?"

"I'm gonna be all right. It's just that he was one of my favorite uncles." He used his left hand to rub his chin in contemplation. "You know, Della, when we were kids, he would always show respect to us. I mean, you know how they used to be. All the other grown-ups always tellin' us to go play, go get something for them, stay outta the front room, don't be around when grown folks are talkin', but Uncle Charles wasn't even like that."

Della creased her lips as she listened.

" I mean, Della, when all the grownups were in the house talkin', he'd be outside helpin' us fix our bikes. He'd tell us these old corny jokes. Yeah, he useta help us train some of them mutts my brother, Doug, useta bring home." A smile came over him, like a shade opening up and inviting in the sunlight. "Every now and then, he would bring home a pretty nice dog like Fee Fee and Drummer. But my favorite was the puppy we called Mikey, after this guy around the corner who had a face like a bulldog."

Della pinched her lip to keep from laughing.

"Della, this boy was ugly! Lawd have Mercy! As a matter of fact, it was Uncle Charles who named the dog after him!" Laughter broke the heaviness in the room. "I'm puzzled, because Uncle Charles took pretty good care of himself. He was gettin' up in age, but he didn't smoke. He drank a little bit. He did like his pork, though. He could sho-nuff eat some ribs and pig's feet."

"Rufus, you ain't gotta be sick to die. All the Lord's gotta do is call you home," Della said. A tranquility came over her countenance. Sincerity was found in her medium-brown eyes. As they walked to the living room, the voice of Walter Cronkite reporting the news came from the walnut-paneled television. Cronkie wore a medium-blue Hickey-Freeman suit, a blue tie with red diagonal stripes, with a traditional white Brooks Brothers shirt. He reported on Nixon, the White House, spiraling inflation, the Middle East unrest, Wall Street, and the war in Vietnam.

Rufus slowly reclined on the plastic-covered sofa and

contemplated his troubles.

"Della, somethin' just ain't right with all of this!" he said. Things just don't add up about Uncle Charles. I think I'm gonna call down there." Della made no comment. She simply continued with the preparation of the chicken sandwiches. She used her steak knife, the one with the mahogany wood handle, to slice the sandwiches in two.

" I think I'll call my cousin, Bob. He'll be straight up with me." His eyes brightened. He went into the kitchen, his shoes accidentally leaving a scuff on the Aztec linoleum. "If you would, just put my sandwich in the refrigerator. I'll get it when I get off the phone."

He dialed the number slowly and carefully. He allowed it to ring five times before he hung up. " I can't believe it. Nobody's home!"

"They're probably with the rest of the family, Rufus. You don't know, maybe they're talkin' 'bout makin' arrangements or somethin'," Della said.

"Yeah, that's possible," he said, restlessly rubbing his chin, looking for something to hold onto. He jumped up out his seat and paced the living room.

"Just try them a little later. Now you can go and eat your sandwich," Della said.

"I ain't really in the mood for eatin' right now. Come on, my uncle just died."

"I understand," she said. There was a lull in her voice and a slight tremble in her left hand as she looked down at the blood-red finish on her fingernails. An acute irritation hung in the air.

"I'm gonna try this number again." A few minutes later, there was a voice on the other end.

"Hello?"

"Hello, how are you doin' Bob?"

"Rufus, my goodness, how you doin?" he said.

"Pretty good, cuz. What's goin' on down there? Della just told me about Uncle Charles. How's everybody holdin' up?"

"As well as expected. Everybody's still shook up. I mean, he wasn't sick or nothin'. We all thought he was in good shape for his age."

"What was it then, Bob?" Was it just his time to go or just what happened?" Rufus asked. Silence came.

"You sittin', Rufus?"

"Yeah. man. Is it that bad?"

"Not as bad as it is deep."

"Talk to me, Bob. Let me know what's goin' on."

"Rufus, you know how Uncle Charles was, don't you?" he asked.

"Man, stop beatin' 'round the bush! Tell me what you talkin' about!"

"All right. You know Uncle Charles really knew how to save some money. He had a little bit stashed away and some of the people in this town knew it." Bob began to take on a more relaxed tone "This nice-lookin' younger woman from Mobile, Alabama had moved here with her three kids she was raisin' on her own -- two girls and one boy. All three have different fathers and she ain't even got no job and barely a place to stay."

"All right, I'm still with ya', Bob," Rufus said.

" She started goin'to our church and everybody could see through her. I mean, she'd go to church shakin' and switchin' like you wouldn't believe! She'd wear short dresses, high heels, plenty o' makeup. You know the women in this church don't dress like that!"

"Yeah, I'm with ya', Bob, but you can't judge her on account of that."

"It was more than just that, trust me. At first glance, Uncle Charles lost his mind over this woman. I knew he had been kinda lonely since Aunt Lucy died, but I ain't nevva seen him act like that over no woman before!" Bob stopped briefly, then went on. "He just kept on sayin' that he had to have her. She heard he had some money and that's when she started battin' her eyes at Uncle Charles at church. In no time, she was comin' over usin' his washin' machine and dryer. She didn't have much in that old dump that she stayed in. He started cookin' for her and her kids. They started to spend more and more time together. We knew that it was real trouble when he brought bunk beds in the house for those kids. The boy slept on the couch and hollered and screamed all night long. Come to find out, he was sleepin' in his momma's bed before they went to Uncle Charles' house. So when his mother started bein' with Uncle Charles, he just about had a fit!"

"That's really somethin', Bob. I didn't know all of that was goin' on."

"We didn't even like talkin' about it."

"I can see why."

"That woman was really puttin' it on Uncle Charles. The last time, she got Uncle Charles so worked up, when he started to have sex with her, his heart just gave out and the rescue squad found him layin' on her butt-naked. She was screamin' and shakin' like a leaf! It's almost like she shoulda known that what she was doin' was way too much for him." Rufus was paralyzed. The words were counter to all that he had believed about Uncle Charles.

"Rufus. Rufus, Rufus."

"Yeah, man, I'm still here. That's just a hard one to swallow."

"I know it is, but that's how it happened," Bob said with somber truth. "The funeral is in three days. You think you'll be able to make it?"

"I don't know. I really don't know. I'm not sure if I'll be able to get out of work." There was strain in Rufus' voice.

"Rufus, you can't worry about what's already happened. It's history. You got to stop worryin'. You gotta pray and ask the Lawd to give you strength."

"I know that already," Rufus said. His voice' rose just a few notches. "Hey, Bob, you take care, man. I'ma try to make it to the funeral, but I can't promise anything. It's kinda rough right now, ya know?"

"I know how it is."

"Give the family my love. I'll talk to you later, Bob."

"Take care, Rufus." As he hung up the phone, his eyes went to the ceiling. He felt the need to be saturated, somehow a balm of healing. He tugged on the creases of his Sansabelt slacks, then he began to think. Uncle Charles: his life, his demise, his drives, chemistry and ambition. Rufus thought about his own death, about the lust that seemed to suffocate his soul. He straightened himself up momentarily and then reclined back onto the plastic-covered couch.

The Rose from Sharon

A split second later came a rude knock on the door. Vivian stood there, child in arm, demanding to speak to Della. Rufus' heart jumped out of his chest at the sight and sound. His worst thought had turned into reality. His crotch and underarms dampened and he swallowed hard. He needed to find a hole, something, anything to burrow his entire body into.

"Mrs. Johnson, can I talk to you for a minute?"

"What can I help you with, young lady?"

"I think we should go into the backyard and talk." Vivian said. Her voice was filled with the bitterness of vinegar.

"What a cute little boy you have. What's his name?"

"Vincent." When they reached the backyard, they sat down at the blond wood picnic table. Someone had carved initials into it.

"Mrs. Johnson, my name is Vivian."

"Pleased to meet you, Vivian." Della said, while extending her hand

"Listen, ma'am, I'm not here to cause no trouble. I just need to clear the air and set the record straight. You see, this child here, well, this is your husband's child. I just want him to give me what I'm entitled to. That's all I want, no trouble, just things that Vincent will need." Della smirked, at first in disbelief. Her eyes shot upwards as she snickered.

"You're kidding, right?" she said. She looked at the baby's eyes. "Why you little whore, you. I oughtta kick yo' ass right here and now." Della moved in closer to Vivian, unbridled anger going unchecked.

"Wait a minute! Just wait a minute, Mrs. Johnson. I think it's your husband you need to have a talk with. He just wouldn't leave me alone!" she shouted. Vivian became both frantic and angry all at the same time. "He kept on after me, even after I told him to leave me alone. He wouldn't do it. If you wanna blame someone, blame him. It's all his fault!"

"It still takes two," Della said. She hung her head low. She felt all alone, betrayed, and downtrodden. Her tears streamed down onto the blonde wood. She stared hopelessly into the wooden swirls and discolorations. There were no answers. How could he? How could he?"

"Mrs. Johnson, I'm really sorry. I never meant to hurt you, although I figured it would. I felt you needed to know the truth." Della could not respond, could not think. She wasn't sure what she was feeling. Then guilt crept in. Self-pity made an entrance. She knew it was a messenger from Satan.

All she could do was keep saying, "How could he, how could he," shaking her head after every syllable.

Rufus sat paralyzed, his brow, armpits, chest, and face drenched in sweat. He was not about to run outside and try to stop the story. It might prove an admission of guilt. Vivian's mouth never ceased from telling her story, but Della's ears were now closed to it. She only felt the seething of her own anger. Della quickly rose from the picnic table. Vivian was in quick pursuit. Tears streamed down Della's eyes. She looked at the kitchen table for napkins to dry her eyes. She hesitated for a while, trying to gain control of the trembling of her hand.

"Della? Is that you?" Rufus asked, still sitting in the living room paralyzed by his transgression.

There was no answer.

Once again he hollered, "Della, is that you?" She stared at Vivian and Vivian, in turn, stared back at her. They both were trying to figure a way out of their pain. Rufus called her name once again. She closed her eyes and whispered an inaudible sound. The last syllable in his voice reverberated in her mind. Della ran with haste, grabbed the butcher knife with the mahogany handle, and went with full speed towards the living room. She screamed at the top of her lungs. Rufus' hands went out in front of him.

"Rufus! You No-good Son-of-a Bitch!!" He stayed seated on the sofa, as if glued there. Della kept coming at him, right arm raised, with the butcher knife in it. He wanted to scream, but was unable to. He kept saying, "Della, no!", but nothing would come out. Suddenly, the sound in his voice reappeared. Della planted her feet firmly in front of him, with the tears falling. He stayed paralyzed with fear. Della's eyes appeared beet-red, as if on fire. Rufus began to plead, "Please, Della. Please, I'm sorry. It'll never happen again." Before he could offer up one more plea, she drove the knife all the way into his upper abdomen. The blood spurted

The Rose from Sharon

first out of his mouth, then like a faucet out of his wound. He let out a primal scream. The sound of it was such that it opened his eyes and woke him out of his dream.

"Hey, Della?" He hollered.

"Yeah, Rufus? What's wrong? You in there hollerin' like the house is on fire!"

"I'm all right. I just had the craziest dream. I think I'm ready for that sandwich now."

"I just about heard you snorin' way in here!" Della said.

"I ain't never had a dream like that before. It felt so real." His breathing was at breakneck speed. He looked around and shook his head in disbelief.

"You wanna tell me about it?" Della asked.

"No, no, that's all right." There were remaining portions of fear still evident in Rufus' eyes, like that of a baby shaken by the sound of a loud voice. He cleared his throat and quickly surveyed the living room.

"My Lord, Rufus, you act like somebody was tryin' to kill you or somethin' in this dream. Look at the front of your shirt. It's damp with sweat." The back of his shirt had become moist that it had stuck to the plastic on the sofa. He stood and discovered that his knees were not giving him adequate strength for standing. The pain sent a message to his mind that said, "maybe God's tryin' to tell me somethin'." It reverberated over and over again.

The rain came down with treachery on the August Saturday morning like an Hawaiian shower that yielded the beauty of a rainbow at the end. The tones shimmering peach, plum-purple, mint, blue and gold, arched through the sky with the magnificence of eternal grace, falling down like nectar from Heaven.

Miss Suzie's wasn't too far off now. Rose had already called her the day before to let her know that she wanted to talk to her. At first, Miss Suzie was apprehensive, but she finally conceded. She was going to be as honest with Rose as she knew how to be. Rose knocked three times at the door, but there was no answer. She knocked again.

Finally, "Who is it?"

"It's me Miss Suzie, Rose Johnson."

"Oh yeah, yeah that's right, hold on. Rose could hear the years of anticipation and broken dreams in her voice.

"Good to see you Rose, come on in. How you doin?"

"I'm doin alright and you?"

"I'm fine for an old woman."

"You know, my brother hurt himself not too long ago."

"I'm sorry chile. What kinda trouble was it?"

"Let's just say he messed with the wrong people"

Miss Suzie shook her head and said, "Lawd have mercy, that's too bad."

"It don't make sense for some of theses folks goin around actin the way they do," Miss Suzie said.

"You are right"

"Now chile what's really on yo mind?"

"How's Ricky doin?"

"You know I think he's doin the best that can be expected of him."

"That's good."

"You know I helped raise that boy as if he were my own. When they had no bread or milk, I gave it gladly. When his mama didn't have it to pay the heat bill in the middle of winter, I helped pay it."

"I didn't know that"

"I love that boy as if he was my own, but I won't smother him with pity, because that's not what he needs. He's stronger than you think. He's been a fighter ever since he's been in the world."

"I understand Miss Suzie."

"That boys a fighter. He's had to ever since he was in the world."

At that point, tears were in both of their eyes.

"Also Rose, if you want to know the truth, you gotta be ready to handle it and I ain't real sure if you're ready yet."

A wall of silence then separated the room momentarily.

"Lets start all over Miss Suzie."

"Not a bad idea. You know Rose it seems to me that you have a good heart and that you really care about other people."

"I really do ma'am. I'm saved and I love the Lord. I love His Word. He told us to love our neighbors as ourselves, "Rose said.

The Rose from Sharon

"I like to hear young people when they talk like that, giving God the praise He rightfully deserves."

"Thank you ma'am"

"You know Rose I use to belong to the church. I even sang in the choir. I saw so many folks doin just the opposite of what they preached, I got discouraged. Shouldn't have, but I did."

"That's too bad, but I notice that myself, Rose said.

"Rose, some of those people who shouted the loudest, when you saw them outside of the church house and sometimes right there on the church grounds, they had more Hell in them than the Devil himself."

"That's ashame."

"I got saved when I was seventeen right there on the mourner's bench. I invited the Lord into my life and I ain't been the same sense."

I started out in the Baptist church and when I got saved, and I thought in my own mind that they weren't saved enough. I ended up joinin the sanctified church and met some good folks there, I mean good folks who really loved the Lord and praised Him in the Spirit."

"That's nice, "Rose said.

"But even there Rose. I knew people who would smile in your face and just as soon cut your throat just to look at ya. But the bishop; Bishop Thomas he was one of the most godliest men I ever met."

****

"There ain't really nothing too much bad I can say about Bishop Thomas," Miss Suzie said. "He wasn't perfect, but he tried to live right. I give him the benefit of the doubt, cause some people just ain't fair to preachers. What do I mean? I mean, he was a man just like any other man and some people think that a preacher is supposed to be perfect. Sometimes men do what they shouldn't do. Bishop Thomas was a good man 'cause he practiced what he preached. He believed in bein' sanctified and that's how he lived."

"That's somethin' else," Rose said.

"His life was a good testimony."

"Miss Suzie, I been really considerin' somethin' ever since the last time we talked."

"What's that, chile?" Miss Suzie asked with her hands folded on her lap, coffee stains on her torn apron.

"I just wondered if you ever found out just who Ricky's daddy was?"

"Why does that mean so much to you?"

"I don't really know why. I just know that it's really eatin' at me. I mean, if he's still livin' or if he's around, maybe he might want to help out."

"Girl, you just don't quit do ya'? But, ya' know what? I made a promise to myself and to the Lord that the next time we talked, I was gonna tell you about all of it."

"I'm ready to know, Miss Suzie."

"You ready for this child?"

"I think I am."

"Maybe the reason you can't get that boy outta yo' head is because that boy is your brother."

"What?" Rose gave a heavy sigh. Her disbelief was beyond restraint. She did well in blinking back tears, but they fell anyway. Her breathing became heavy. "I can't believe that. I just can't believe you, Miss Suzie," she said looking at the ground, while shaking her head, partly in denial, partly in shame.

"Well, chile, I ain't got no reason to lie to ya'. Sometimes when you ain't ready to deal with the truth, it's best that you leave it alone." There was a sharpness in her words.

"How do you know this, Miss Suzie?" she asked. Miss Suzie simply looked at her, as if in utter shock.

"Chile, what do you mean, 'how do I know?' I done lived in this neighborhood and in this house for a whole lot of years. I know a whole lot about a whole lot. I've seen a lot. Chile, I done seen and heard things that'll make your toes curl. I ain't no stranger to none of this."

"I just can't believe it," Rose continued to say over and over again as if her words had been put into a spin cycle. She rubbed on her brow. Her head hung low as if just informed of death. Miss Suzie's words pummeled her mind.

"I know it's hard to take and you might not really understand right now, but you have to remember that your dad is a man. Remember what I said about men?"

"What's that supposed to mean?"

"Your dad is a man. That means he got the nature of a man. Sometimes they get greedy and try to get more than they can chew on!" Rose simply remained silent.

"Even a good man gets caught up in things that he ain't got no business gettin' caught up in."

"What are you tryin' to do, justify my dad's actions?"

"No I'm not tryin' to justify anything. I'm just tellin' it like it is. A man is always gonna have some lust in his heart."

"Well, just because a man thinks about this stuff, don't mean he should act on it!" Rose said.

"That's right, but everybody don't think like that. The happy man is the one who might think about it, but don't do it cause he know that if you just hold out, there's joy in the morning."

"I know that. I just can't believe that he could do something like this to my ma." Rose said.

"I ain't got the answer for that. All I know is that it happened. It can't be undone. You ain't got to go and tell your dad that you know, and I forbid you to tell your mom."

"Why?" Rose asked. Her brow frowned in frustration.

"You think your mother knowing about this will do any good in helping their marriage?"

"No."

"That's right. I know this is hard, but as much as you can, try and act like nothing ever happened. As for Ricky, try to treat him as a brother whenever you see him and put this pain behind you." Rose stared at her with intensity. The deep blackness of her eyelashes became damp with her tears.

"I feel bad now for telling you this, but I knew that you wouldn't let it go."

"All I got to say is, do you think you could just put it behind you if it were you?"

" I don't know, Rose. I don't know," Miss Suzie said. Miss

Suzie's eyes suddenly became bloodshot from strain and sadness. For Rose, the news permeated her emotions like a harpoon enters the slippery gray flesh of a killer whale. Rose looked into Miss Suzie's eyes. Although she saw her own sorrow, there was a sincerity in her eyes that Rose could not deny.

"I'm tellin' you, Rose, and I mean what I say, keep what I told you to yourself," Miss Suzie said in a voice full of the frigid agony of a thousand Alaskan winters. Her words jangled Rose's mind.

"Yes, Miss Suzie. I'll do what you asked. Have a good day."

"You do the same. Stop by anytime," Miss Suzie said. Rose walked out the door with the weight of uninvited knowledge laid open on her shoulders.

A year and a half had passed. It was now the spring of '73. There was a renewed spirit lingering heavily in the air. Jesse's track career was hitting full stride. Rufus had returned to work. Rose had become the second-in-command of the school newspaper. Larry had found some level of healing, but could not find the strength to say "no" to the streets.

Jesse was entering his sophomore year at the state college. He was able to make the trip in approximately 57 minutes from home, whenever he drove his '68 faded yellow Datsun Corona. It was a nimble five-speed number with short napped carpet, like that of a well coifed poodle.

Jesse's major course of study was communications. It was a cushion move that would ensure a presentable grade point average throughout the school year. He figured that if the Olympics didn't become a reality, then with his love of music, he could become successful in the radio industry.

His nose was being opened by some of the most prime cuts of young femininity that he had ever known. They were from small towns, as well as metro stations from Michigan, Ohio, Maryland, Illinois. He even met a young lady from Trinidad. But he still found time to spend with Rose.

His track and field conditioning demanded much from his body. In time, his thigh and calf muscles resembled that of lean, taut brown sinew. His biceps grew well-defined. His shoulders had developed into almost perfect horizontal planes. Although he had access to the

The Rose from Sharon

most advanced weight lifting machinery, he never abandoned free weights. They allowed for less restriction and yielded a beauty and cut to the muscle that the new equipment just wouldn't .

As that season closed, it was no great surprise to anyone when he won the Most Valuable Player award. At the ceremony his mother was beside herself with tears. The greater victory was that he was the first freshman in the school's history to win the award.

Although Jesse stood tall on the track field, his schoolwork left something to be desired. But he promised his mother that the next year would be an improvement. A year of college had been completed and Jesse felt the pride that a father feels when he holds his newborn child.

He packed up all the books he was unable to sell, along with his denim and polyester bell-bottoms and T-shirts, as well as his wide-lapeled dressier shirts. He packed his sweaters and well-worn socks.

Particular care was taken when it came to handling his musical collection. He proceeded to package up his Al Green, *I'm Still in Love With* You and *Let's Stay Together*" albums, The Temptations *Greatest Hits* and *All Directions,*" *The Mack* by Willie Hutch, and *Superfly* by Curtis Mayfield.

He thought about the eternal fluidness of Marvin Gaye's *What's Goin' On*, and *Let's Get It On* albums, as he placed them in a cardboard box. He looked at the simplicity of Gaye's *Super Hit*" album cover. It depicted him in an animated comic book's, hero regalia with a beautiful brown-skinned sister being taken upwards in the sky, wrapped in the arms of safety. It was music that helped motivate him before a meet would began. He listened to Tom Jones' *Fever Zone* and the soulful voice of Bobby Womack, that would send him into another territory of thinking when he listened to <u>Close to You</u> on his *Communication* album.

He packed albums by Otis Redding, Wilson Pickett, The Jazz Crusaders, Les McCarn, Jerry Butler, Etta James, Johnnie Taylor. Along with these, he added the pure soul of Sam Cooke and the unquenchable fire of James Brown. These albums were all scratched, almost beyond use from continuous play.

Rufus was pleased, as well as relieved, to be back to work. When he returned, he approached work with caution. His body couldn't afford a relapse.

Vivian went full speed ahead with her life. She also continued to keep their son out of Rufus's life. She started dating one of the hitters on the varsity team by the name of Larnell Taylor. He was a stocky young man with a bull neck, the strength of a lion and, arguably, the mind of a chimpanzee.

The situation put Rufus's teeth on edge. Every time he would see them together he felt the underpinnings of hatred, grief and jealousy. It gave Rufus a feeling of powerlessness, of being caged in. Vivian had heightened his sense of masculinity, while it was Della who presented the portrait of true reality to him.

Every evening at the dinner table, Rufus's attempts at inviting conversation would come to naught. Della's only reply would be, "Everything's all right" or "I just don't feel up to talkin' right now." His guilt was becoming murder.

One Saturday evening, his mind almost turned inside out. At 6:45 there came a knock on the door. A lush, early summer breeze was blowing at a consistent pace. The emerald-green leaves on the trees shimmered in the light wind. Rose was sitting on the couch with her feet tucked underneath her legs. She wore a pair of lime-green cotton slacks with a short-sleeved top with a tapestry print. Jesse sat on the couch next to her.

On the second knock, Rose went to the door. It was Vivian and Larnell. Rufus was sitting at the kitchen table putting stamps on the envelopes for the electric, gas and telephone bills.

"What's happenin', girl?" Vivian said, her hips swaggering and voluptuous.

"Not much. What's goin' on with you?" Rose asked.

"I'm doin' good."

"How you doin', Larnell?"

"Fine 'n you?" He answered in a bass voice.

"Come to me, little guy," Rose said, as Vivian gently handed her child into Rose's waiting arms.

Uncanny thoughts of fear shot through Rufus's mind in the span of split seconds. He sat in his chair and contemplated heavily whether or not he should even move. His kidneys went into distress as he listened to their small talk. He continued to wonder to himself: what nerve.

"So what time do you think ya'll gonna be back?" Rose asked.

"Probably around eleven. It shouldn't be much later than that. We gonna do it up tonight 'cause Rose, you ain't gonna believe what happened to me today." Vivian said with unusual exuberance in her voice.

"Well, what's up, Vivian?"

"We got engaged!"

"Engaged? Congratulations. I'm happy for you, Vivian!"

"He told me he's been savin' up all summer for my ring. Ain't it nice?" Rose looked down at a quarter-carat marquis-cut diamond with minimal flaws. There was a brilliance to it, albeit with imperfections that only a skilled geologist could detect.

"It's beautiful, Vivian!"

"Thanks," she said, as she raised her hand and used her index finger to wipe away tears. Although happy about the occasion, Rose couldn't help but feel empathy for Larnell. He would be in for a challenge every day of his married life. Rufus's mind flickered like a weak light bulb. He stood up from his chair, his knees stiff. He exhaled heavily and peered out the window. He was defeated by the realization that Rose would be unknowingly baby-sitting her own brother.

Rose was baby-sitting so that Vivian and Larnell could go out to dinner and a movie. Rufus seethed inwardly. He thought about his feelings for Vivian; the gifts -- monetary and material -- his soul. He thought about the clothing, the jewelry, the roses, the shoes, the wafer-thin, mint-filled chocolates that she so loved. These thoughts trudged through his mind like a backhoe breaks up earth.

"Hey! Young-ass nigga! What you doin' in my house with her? You ain't even got no business bein' with her!" Everyone in the room stared in disbelief.

"Excuse me, sir? Why you talkin' to me like that? What've I done to you?" Larnell asked.

"Don't ask me no questions and don't get smart with me in my house! I will whip yo' ass!" Rufus hollered.

"I ain't here for no trouble. Maybe we should just go, Vivian."

"Do whatever," she said.

"Now you ain't goin' nowhere without an ass whippin' first," Rufus said, as he walked over to Larnell and grabbed him by the collar. Larnell pushed Rufus over the coffee table.

Rufus hollered, "My back! My back!"

Jesse intervened between the two. "That's enough, ya'll!!"

"What's wrong with you, Daddy? Why would you do something like that?"

"I got my reasons."

"No, there was no reason for that," Rose said.

"We'll see you later, Rose," Vivian said, as she and Larnell made haste in leaving.

"I hope ya'll have fun," Rose said, as she closed the door behind them while holding the baby. Rufus's eyes were empty. His face was as blank as the serenity of still waters. Everything inside of him was ravaged and made complicated with pain and torment. Had it come to this? He now felt humiliated, embarrassed, pummeled.

"Hey Rose, it's gettin' a little late. Maybe I should go. I'll see you later," Jesse said. The climate of the room was more than he could handle. He lifted himself off of the couch and touched Rose with tenderness on the arm. He closed the door with extra caution.

After fifteen minutes, Della arrived home. As usual, sadness was upon her. Rufus had a look of concern. Rose felt the urgency of her mother's sadness. "Ma, you look like something's wrong."

"There is," Della said.

"What is it?" Rose asked.

"Sister Gaines and I were just sittin' and talkin', sharin' recipes, you know, family matters. All of a sudden the phone rang. Her granddaughter was on the line, just cryin' and hollerin' like the world was about to end. Sister Gaines finally got her to calm down. That's when she told her grandmother that her mother, Trudy, had shot herself in the head.

"Oh my God, not Trudy! She was a good girl!" Rufus said.

"They tried to revive her but there was no hope. It was too late. "

"Lawd have mercy, that's a shame!" Rufus said.

The Rose from Sharon

****

Trudy was a standout. She excelled in math, figuring seven-digit problems with pleasure. She possessed beautiful, light hazel-green eyes and medium brown hair that went well with her desert-tan complexion. She had a promising career with the First Bank of Detroit until she was convicted of embezzlement. That cost her five years of her life in the Michigan State Women's Prison.

Prior to that, she was living a charmed life in the Outer Drive area of Detroit in an apartment laid out with burgundy wall-to-wall carpeting. She had a cherry wood dining room set and velour living room furniture done in silver with a brocade design. She drove a brand-new Pontiac Granville. It was white with white leather interior, white vinyl top, power moon roof, air conditioning, power seats, power steering, power brakes, and power windows.

While she was incarcerated, she became a savage victim of her own beauty and endured gang rape and constant molestation. Six months following her release, Trudy was under strict psychiatric care and medication. It was ineffective because it made her moody, unpredictable, and at times, promiscuous.

This left her prey to the slick-talking street brothers, who knocked down the door of her heart without mercy. The one that she fell hard for was Tommy Hanson, a fast-talking, ball playing brother. He told her that he loved her. She believed him. He told her that they would one day marry. She believed him. He told her that no other woman in the world mattered. She believed him. Friends would consistently tell her about the other woman. She refused to hear it. They stumbled recklessly through four years, the longest of any affair that she knew.

One Saturday, he came over with another woman. If that wasn't painful enough, he beat Trudy in front of her. As the tears fell from her eyes, Tommy and the other woman slammed the door and went down the stairs. As Tommy went to start the ignition in his dark blue Cadillac, a shot rang out as he turned the ignition key.

It stopped him cold, a jolt of nervous electricity shooting up his back. Disbelief took over, as he heard Trudy's daughter's cries coming from the second floor of the building. He couldn't bear it.

He simply drove off in the fury of his own madness.

****

The next day during church service, the pastor's sermon dealt with "reaping and sowing." It cut Rufus, as with a two-edged sword. He sat back in the pews waiting for the punishment to cease. His soul languished. A river of agony rushed through to the other side. At the end of the sermon, Rufus didn't waste much time hanging around. He fled as soon as possible. When they arrived home, Rose looked at her father. She seemed to connect with his misery, but she wouldn't sympathize with it. Rose stared until it became uncomfortable.

There was a newspaper article from two days back that she wanted to take a look at. She looked in all the rooms downstairs then went upstairs to look in Larry's room, knowing that he always kept old newspapers. As she went into the room and switched on the light, a gunshot shattered the glass of the room's east window. A voice that seemed to bark from hell shouted out, "I told you we'd get you! This is just a warning, Larry! Get us our money, or we gonna kill yo' ass!" Within seconds, the gray '68 Impala shot like a rocket down the street. Rufus and Della darted up the stairs.

"Rose, are you all right?" Della asked.

"I'm just scared." The trajectory of the bullet made a hole in the ceiling. A sense of disbelief and fear permeated the room. "Mama, just what is Larry up to?" Rose asked.

"I don't know, Rose. I really don't know." They all just looked at one another.

"We got to do something about Larry and we need to do it quick," Della said. "We gotta get our heads outta the sand and stop actin' like ain't nothin' wrong with him." The telephone interrupted her in mid-sentence.

"Hello, Ma'am, may I speak with a Mrs. Johnson?" the voice said.

"This is she."

"Mrs. Johnson, my name is Nurse Kirchner." At those words, Della's heart raced. Her breathing convulsed. She tried desperately to dispel the human tendency to assume the worst, but she couldn't.

"What's wrong, Nurse Kirshner?" she asked.

"It's your son, Larry. He was in a bad car accident."

"Lawd, no, no. How much am I s'posed to take? Is he all right?"

"He's currently in intensive care with severe internal bleeding, a sprained neck, facial cuts, and a broken right forearm and right leg," she said. Della's heart ached like human flesh being skillfully turned back by a single edged razor and then having rubbing alcohol poured onto the exposed inner flesh.

"What's wrong, Della?" Rufus asked.

"Larry was in a car accident. We need to get to the hospital."

"Lawd Jesus! How bad is he?"

"Bruised, broken up. We gotta get to the hospital." Della forgot to even hang up the phone. And as they went out the door, the voice of Nurse Kischner could still be heard coming through the receiver.

"Hello? Hello? Mrs. Johnson? Are you there?"

As they approached the emergency room, a grievous fog grabbed them. "Where is Nurse Kischner?" Della asked the woman at the desk. She paced back and forth nervously.

"She's attending someone right now, Ma'am. May I help you?"

"My son was in a bad car accident and we need to see him!" The tone in her voice rose.

"In that case, you go right back there, ma'am. Just take a right turn around the corner and follow the sign." The third curtain that they peaked behind held Larry. Nurse Kirshner quickly went to them, ushering them out to inform and confer.

"So you are Mr. and Mrs. Johnson?" she asked.

"Yes," Rufus said.

"I'm Nurse Kirshner. Your son was seriously injured. It's hard to tell the extent of his internal injuries. We are running tests now," she said.

"That's good."

"The police report is not complete yet, but what they do know is that there was no other vehicle involved. They're still not sure what made his car swerve into that buckeye tree. Blood tests have shown through that there was alcohol and traces of marijuana in his system. To what degree, it's not real clear yet," she said. They then went to look in on Larry. They found him unconscious. There were scratches, mainly on his face. His lip appeared to be swollen. His leg and arm were in casts. A sullen gust of wind came through the room.

As Rufus looked at his son, his breathing became heavy. His mouth was parched. An aura of defeat entrapped him in something that he felt was out of his grasp. He clenched his fist in anger and disgust.

"Why did it take this?" Over and over, his mind asked this question. Overcome with a tirade of emotions, Rufus retreated to the lobby in order to recalibrate. His soul felt abandoned, like a heart that has no blood to pump through it.

****

The next night, Rufus lay in bed with his eyes open. Sleep wanted nothing to do with him. He feared that his demons would return. In spite of his fear, he remained in prayer. Shortly thereafter, he began experiencing pain in his arm, his leg and in certain internal organs. An unwanted heat began to go into those areas characterizing a life all of its own. It was trying to suffocate him. He wanted to scream out, but was unable to. He prayed its departure, not knowing that those areas of pain were the phantom projections of his son's injuries.

At around 3:45, in the stark blackness of the early morning, he rose out of his bed. He went downstairs and sat in his favorite chair for comfort. He went into the bathroom and turned the faucet to lukewarm. It took him four splashes to the face to get him into a zone of humanity. His blood vessels were open and his pores were closed.

He walked back to his bedroom and slipped out of his Fruit of the Loom underwear and replaced them with a clean pair. He put on a brown pair of polyester slacks, a New England fisherman-style sweater, brown ribbed socks and an old pair of wing-tipped shoes, heels worn to a wedge. He tiptoed towards the door, but Della asked, "Where you think you goin'?"

Her voice startled him. His startled heart gyrated out of its natural rhythm. "What? I thought you were sleep. You scared the heck out of me!"

"So where ya' goin', Rufus?"

"For a ride. I can't sleep. I need to clear my head. Ain't no need in keepin' you up tossin' and turnin'."

"You ain't gonna keep me from my sleep." she said.

"I don't want to. I just need to get out and get some fresh air." He went swiftly to the Pontiac. He used his glove to wipe away the slight frost that had formed on the windows. He pulled out of the driveway and drove down the street to his old elementary school. He momentarily parked his car, looked at the playground and thought about the times at recess he used to enjoy playing kickball.

He drove by the old neighborhood and looked at the house where he grew up. He thought about his mother's cornbread, collard greens, and fried chicken; how his aunts and uncles would all assemble and talk and laugh and languish in the love of one another. He drove away, but a part of him still remained in that house, which contained his days of youth.

As he drove on, he continued to repeat to himself, "How could I let God down the way that I have, and then not confess it to my own family and church?" He looked at the beads of dew that had formed on the dense grass. "How can I continue to hide this thing?"

He thought about his sons, Ricky and Larry. What would become of him? He chastised himself for the things that Larry had done. He thought, "if only I'd spent more time with him, talked to him more." Then maybe it would have not come to such a matter.

He drove again, this time ending up at the river, a place of solitude where he and his friends went fishing as children. They'd caught perch, walleye, and blue gill. Rufus sat there until he saw a peek of gold slowly rise out of the eastern sky. His shoulder blades and lower back were weary. He turned the ignition key and started for home. His head was held low as he walked through the front door. As he looked up, his eyes met his wife, who was sitting in the corner chair, wearing a pink robe and pink slippers. She said not a word. Her eyes were filled with sadness and strain. When he glanced at the stairway, he was confronted by the piercing gaze of his daughter. Her head was slightly tilted to the side as if prepared for confrontation.

"Where you been, Daddy?"

"I been out drivin', sweetie, just thinking about things," he said as he attempted to hide his guilt.

"So you got a lot of things on your mind?" she asked.

"Yeah, I do. I think about you, your Mom, your brother. I think about a lot of things." He tried not to be remiss in greeting his wife. "Oh, Della, how you doin'? Can you do me a favor?"

"What?" she asked.

"Call the job. Tell them what happened, you know, that our son was in a very serious accident and because of his condition, I won't be able to come into work today."

"What's wrong with you? You can't do that?" she asked.

"Yeah, I can do it, but I asked you to do it, if you would. I'm just in no condition to talk to them right now," he said in a weak and unsure voice.

"All right, Rufus."

She went into the kitchen to make the call, and to heat a pot of water for coffee. "Well, Rose, you goin' to school today?"

"Yes. I was planning on it."

A spirit of truth fell upon Rufus. "I feel some responsibility for your brother's accident," Rufus said.

"Why do you say that? How can you be responsible for Larry's accident?" Rose asked.

"You're right. I wasn't there, but in a way I was, because I am a part of your brother, as well as you."

"I know that, but how does that make you responsible for his accident?"

"Rose, I'm gonna try and make it clear to you. Remember when you were younger and ya'll saw so little of me because I was workin' all the time?"

"Yes, I remember. I used to have plays in grade school and school concerts and you could never make it, 'cause you were at work," she said with sadness and regret.

"Now you understand what I'm tryin' to say. I worked overtime to try and make things better for ya'll. I worked when both of ya'll were young. Larry wasn't like you were."

"How?"

"When you were small, you used to read a lot for a young kid. I liked that in you. But when Larry was small, sometimes he would go for days without speaking. I'd whip him. I don't know now if I was right or wrong for that. He still won't speak."

"I didn't know that, Daddy."

"He used to fight with other kids and cause all sorts of problems in the neighborhood. I'd whip him 'til I couldn't whip him no more. He got older and smarter. He was gettin' too big for whippins. Before long, I was workin' seven days a week, 70 hours. I couldn't be here. I could have said No to the overtime, but the money got too good." He stopped momentarily, abruptly.

"I found out too late that none of the trouble stopped. Why am I saying all this? You know about the things your brother did. I don't need to tell you."

"No, Daddy. Not all of it. He had his friends and I had mine." she said.

"It had just about reached a point where I was sick and tired of all the fussin' and just about gave up on him. I cared about him. I just didn't know what to do about him. The pain of it was killin' me on the inside. The only way I knew to make it better was to keep on workin', so I did. But what you fail to realize was, my family was crumblin' right in front of me. Your Mom needed me, Larry needed me, you needed me. I just wanted to do my own thing."

"Don't be so hard on yourself about everything, Dad. You have to just leave it in God's hands and He'll work it out the way it's supposed to be," Rose said.

"I know. That's really good to hear you say that, Rose."

"I said it because I really do believe it. I better start getting ready for school now."

"Yeah, it's getting late." He scratched the back of his neck and messaged his eyebrows with his left index finger and thumb. There was a brief pause before he turned and walked out the door for air. He paced back and forth on the porch, waiting for peace to come. Without his jacket on, the air was punishing. As the frigid air hit him, he felt like he was in a fight. How do you measure the pain of a punch to the abdomen?

Fatigue encompassed him. The whites of his eyes were the color of unripe tangerines. He was headed back into the house when a green Ford Torino that had been parked at the corner pulled out quickly. A voice rang out from the driver's seat. "Man, you better think hard about your son!"

As Rufus turned his head to respond, a bullet from a .22 fired from the car and grazed the side of his head, drawing blood. His kidneys half emptied. He ran into the house and through the living room. His chest pounded. Guilt swarmed him like a bee's nest. Della came out of the kitchen.

"What in the world?"

"I been shot, Della. I been shot."

"Lawd have mercy! Who did that to ya', the same hoodlums that shot through the window? What they tryin' to do, kill the whole family?" Della asked. She was upset, but fought to try and contain it.

Rufus grabbed a Kleenex from the living room coffee table and wiped the blood from his temple.

"Let me take you to the hospital, Rufus. You don't know how bad it might be!" she said.

"I'm gonna try and hold still," Rufus said while bending over for Della to place bandages on the wound.

"You need to go to the hospital! You don't know how bad it could become!"

"That's my ear you shoutin' in!" he shouted back as they drove to the hospital.

Inside he was saying," Thank you, Jesus, for saving me!"

"You ought be thankin' God that He spared you, Rufus," she said.

"You think I ain't thankful? You better believe that I am!"

"You actin' kinda calm." she said.

Chapter 8

"You think I wasn't scared when I realized that bullet hit me? Hell yeah, I was scared. Scared to death is more like it. I just thank God you ain't callin' the undertaker right now. You see, God still got His hands on me. He's still got some work left for me to do down here."

Not sure what to make of what he was saying, Della just looked at him as if he were brought forth from the dead.

"I just feel real good right now because I really feel that God's hand is on me. It's just a doggone shame that it took a whole bunch of junk to show me that I ain't nothing!"

Della remained unconvinced. She laughed softly at the confession and said to herself, "If getting shot will make him talk like this, he needs to catch a bullet every day." But in reality, she knew that this righteous fear had no intention of taking root.

"See, it's not all that important what I've done or haven't done. What's important right now is that I'm alive and I'ma try to do the right thing from now on."

"What makes you think that whatever you've done is not important? It's important to me!"

When they looked at Larry, they sank deeper into the abyss. As Rufus looked at his son, uncertainty was striving to weaken his fortitude. He began to dwell on the scripture, *By His steps we are healed.*

The doctor entered the room with an innate authority. Although preoccupied in some thought of prior importance, he hid it in the spirit of professionalism.

"I'm sorry I wasn't here earlier when you came to see Larry," he said.

"We know you're a busy man, Doctor," Della said.

"Yes I am. I know you're very concerned about Larry, but he is making progress. The progress is a little bit slow, but it's still progress."

"Well, progress is progress, Della" Rufus said. She didn't engage him, except for the vicious rolling of her eyes.

"He's responding well to everything and is cooperating just fine. But, of course he's still in a great deal of pain and we are trying to keep that to a minimum through medication. The down side of the medication is that it makes him sleep a lot. So overall, it looks as if he's out of any real impending danger, as far as I can see."

"Well praise the Lord for that," Della said.

"But one thing does concern me," the doctor said. "I was talking to Officer Daniels before you came in."

"What'd he want?" Rufus asked. It made him want to straighten up his own life that much more. The pain that his son was suffering made him see the sting of sin and death more clearly. His son's agony was leading him to righteousness. His suffering became a balm of healing.

The medication that they gave Larry left him heavily sedated. As a result, it would be several hours before he would awaken. Rufus and Della sat down and waited for some change to occur. As they sat, neither spoke a word to the other. They sat in stupefied silence.

Chapter 9

Rose found concentrating in class that next day to be impossible. Her brother's pain haunted her and pierced at her focus. The study of "Maslov's Hiearchy of Needs" left her in a pure quandary in sociology class. She was upset at herself for letting something master her that was seemingly easily mastered. Without a doubt, she knew that on any other day, it would be conquered. But given the circle of events, she was left wanting. Something anticipatory haunted her. She couldn't feel anything in her soul, save despair. She had an encompassing need to call Jesse.

At 3:44 pm she arrived home after school. By 3:47 she was on the phone dialing Jesse. It rang three times, but no one answered. She tried again fifteen minutes later, but still, no one answered. She felt a starving in her heart to just hear his voice. After she drank a glass of red Kool-Aid, she tried again. After two rings, Jesse picked up the receiver. "Hello."

"And just where have you been?" she asked.

"I was at the library. What's up with you comin' at me like that?" Silence sapped the air out of them both.

"I'm sorry, I shouldn't have said that," she said.

"What's the matter with you?" Jesse said.

"I don't know where to start. Larry's in the hospital. He done tore his car up. My dad, aw man, Jesse, he's lost his mind. I don't even have time to start in on him."

"What is it?"

"I've just had a bad day. It just seems like my family is coming apart at the seams!"

"Rose, you can't get yourself worked up over people who just don't wanna do right."

"But this is my family!"

"I know that. But they're also grown. You can't make grown people do what they don't wanna do," Jesse said.

"I called you thinking it would make me feel better. You makin' me feel worse," Rose said with a sense of heartfelt regret.

"I ain't trying to bring you down. I'm just bein' real with you," he said.

"Bein' real with me? Is that what you call it?"

"That's all I'm doin', baby. When you start seein' things the way they really are, then you'll be able to deal with them a lot better."

"So now I can't deal with things?"

"That's not what I meant. You're taking what I'm saying the wrong way," he said.

"Well, how else am I s'pose to take it?"

"I refuse to argue with you, Rose."

"I'm not gonna argue with you either, Jesse."

"It's been a rough day, Rose, but things will get better. I just know they will," Jesse said.

There was a whimper in Rose's voice. "Are you alright, Rose?"

"Yeah, I'm gonna be just fine."

"I'm sorry if I said anything to upset you. I really didn't mean it." While they were talking, Jesse watched TV, splitting his interest between the two.

"Maybe I should get movin' now, Rose. I'll talk to you later."

"Alright then, goodbye," Rose said.

He turned the channels, back and forth, forth and back. His mind slowly dissolved of all self-absorbing thought. He went from a television revival to a situation comedy to a crime drama and then back to the television revival. As he listened to the evangelist, the preaching engrossed him. It wasn't that he was speaking words that he hadn't heard before, but they had a hidden impact, an unforeseeable force, an innate spirituality that was filled with a keen supernatural power. The preaching touched Jesse at the very core of his heart. As the evangelist spoke of the magnificence of God, the description of His awesomeness dwarfed Jesse. It made him feel protected and important. A warmth emerged inside of him. The preacher then asked the question," If you died tonight, where would you spend eternity?" The question silenced all sound in Jesse's mind. It engaged the inner fiber of his soul. Suddenly, the tragedy of sin seemed as if it could be extinguished.

O death, where is thy sting, O grave, where is thy victory?

Jesse started now to think about his own life, its twists, turns and times of loneliness; the moments of passion for a dream; the days of not caring either way, of being in so much trouble, but not knowing who would bring him out. Somehow, someway, behind the shadows of life's murky seas, victory was waiting. During these times, there was no doubt in his mind that it was the outstretched hand of God that turned his darkness into day.

The preacher asked, "For those who aren't sure that once they leave this life, they'll see Heaven, believe in your hearts and repeat this prayer with me."

Lord Jesus, I confess to you that I am a sinner. But I no longer want to live a life with sin planned in it. I acknowledge that Jesus died for my sins. I would ask that you forgive me of my sins and cleanse me. Right now Lord, I invite you to come into my life as Savior and Lord and I will live my life for you from this moment forth. In Jesus' name. Amen.

After Jesse repeated this prayer, he instantly felt a heavy burden lifted. He became immersed in an aura of peace. He felt the presence of overwhelming love. Nothing had ever taken him over like this before. A newness. A freshness. Power. Anointing. Holy ghost. SALVATION.

The preacher said, "If you repeated that prayer, if you were sincere about that prayer and meant it in your heart, then you are now saved." Jesse didn't need to be convinced.

"Now if you have just accepted Jesus Christ as your savior, you must understand some things about salvation. It is a gift from God. You can't earn it, you can't work for it. Salvation is not based on how you feel, it's based on faith," the preacher said. At that, an enormous roar of "amens" went into the chilled air of the stadium.

As the cheers slowly subsided, the preacher said, "Some may shout, some may cry. Some might raise their hands in praise. Some may not feel anything. But it's not so important what you feel. What's important is - did you believe?"

Jesse immediately rose to dial the phone. It rang twice before someone answered.

"Hello."

"Hey, Momma, how you doin'?"

"Just fine. How you doin', Jesse?"

"Mom, I'm doin' great! I feel fantastic! I just accepted the Lord into my life. I just got saved!"

"THANK YOU JESUS. THANK YOU JESUS!!!" his mother cried. "I prayed and prayed and prayed for you, boy. I know you didn't get into a lot of trouble. I just wanted things for you to be better. I always prayed that God would be the head of your life."

"Momma, all I know is that I feel good. I mean real good. I just wish I would've listened and done it a long time ago," he said.

"Son, I love ya' and I'm proud of ya'."

"I love you too, Mom."

"You take care, Jesse."

"Alright, Mom. I'll be talking to ya' later."

There came a rude knock at the door. It shook his sanctuary.

"Who is it?"

"It's me, man. What's up?" The voice belonged to Jimmy McDaniel, a comrade who was in the early stages of drunkenness via the wickedness of poorly fermented wine. His voice almost sent Jesse into another realm of thought.

"Come on in, Jimmy. The door is open."

"What's happenin', Jesse?" he asked as he extended his hand to give Jesse five.

"I'm doin' good, Jimmy. How 'bout you?"

"Feelin' no pain, bro. Feelin' no pain." Jesse beheld him simply shook his head in disgust.

"Man, what am I gonna do with you, Jimmy?"

"Ha, ha, funny man, funny," Jimmy said, with a frisky attitude that transcended even his state of drunkenness.

"So what's up, Jesse, you goin' out to party with me or what?"

The Rose from Sharon

"I don't need that kinda high anymore, Jimmy. I just got saved and right now I'm high on Jesus. No alcohol or weed has ever felt as good as this. I just wish I would have accepted the Lord much sooner than this. I could've saved myself a lot of headaches!"

"I'm really glad to hear that, man. That's a good thing. Yeah - that's a good thing," Jimmy said.

"It's the best decision I've ever made in my life."

"But are you sure you don't wanna go out one more time for old time's sake?"

"Yeah man, that's a turned page in my life. That stuff there can't do nothing for me anymore." Jesse hesitated because of the essence of the moment. "So when're you gonna make a change, Jimmy?" All of the energy in the room took an immediate pause.

"What? You tryin' to put me on a guilt trip, man? I know I drink too much and party too much. I guess I have myself to blame. Jesse, man, I'll tell ya'. Some of the head trips my old man took my mother and me through as a kid were really something. I get high a lot of the time just to forget the pain," he said.

"Jimmy, you can't drink your problems away. You can't smoke your problems away. You can't shoot 'em away. Guess what? When you come down from that high, those same problems will be looking you square in the face. In fact, when you get high, you've made the problem worse, because now you've also got to deal with a hangover," Jesse said.

"Hey, I know everything you're sayin' is right. I just got to put it in practice."

"What about right now, man? None of us know what tomorrow holds. You may not even be here," Jesse warned. Jimmy raised his eyes upward. His face was the epitome of both loneliness and strange betrayal.

"Check this out, Jesse. One time Dad slapped my mom real hard on the left side of her face, then pushed her down some stairs. I was so mad I called him a 'bastard.' He put a knife to my throat and told me 'You already know the same thing'll happen to you if I ever hear you call me that again.' Then with a wicked smile on his face, he slapped me in the mouth and made my lip bleed."

"That's really messed up, Jimmy. But don't be hard on yourself because of your father's stupidity. It ain't your fault."

"Yeah, I believe you're right, but I don't think I've ever been that scared in my life, Jesse. He used to always tell me I couldn't make it and that I wasn't no good, even when I was bringin' home As and Bs from school. I been told I ain't no good for so long, I really started to believe that I ain't meant to go to Heaven, man," he said as his left foot trembled in a syncopated rhythm.

"That's not true at all, Jimmy. If that was true, Jesus would have never come to die for our sins. He died for everybody, man," Jesse said.

"You ain't tryin' to be holier-than-thou now, are you?"

"No man, I'm just telling you like it is 'cause I used to be where you are, as far as doubt is concerned." Jesse said.

"Oh, yeah.?

"I mean, it's based all on faith, man. It's not something you can work for or earn."

"Oh yeah?" Jimmy said.

"Yeah, man, I mean when I heard the preacher preachin', I felt like the word was just for me and by faith, I accepted it." His words almost pricked Jimmy into sobriety. They hit him with the same intensity as if he were walking for miles within the terror of a hailstorm.

It quickened him, but he shied from its beckoning. But he knew that something would eventually have to be done about the position of his soul.

"Hey man, I'm happy for ya', but I gotta go. Later on, Jesse." Jimmy moved with fury out of the room. The latch on the maple wood door clicked like an empty revolver. Jesse's mind languished on the obvious conviction that permeated through Jimmy like the effectiveness of the perfect antibiotic.

Jesse said aloud to himself, "It's just a matter of time." Within an hour, Jesse was in bed. Not too long after the sheets adjusted themselves to his body temperature, he fell into a coma-like sleep. He would have slept on, but was awakened by a massive sound. Upon awakening, his movements were slow and calculated. He went to his knees to thank God for a good night's sleep and for waking him up with joy in his heart. A brisk shower followed. He proceeded

The Rose from Sharon

into a light workout that consisted of stretching and calisthenics. He followed with twenty pushups, breathed, then followed that with twenty-five more pushups. After a two-minute rest, he did 50 more pushups.

Just after finishing up his workout, a knock at the door interrupted his concentration. "

Who is it?"

"Open the door, Jesse." The voice had the tint of drama attached to it, the kind of drama that Jesse wanted to avoid. It was Mikies "The Snake" Edwards. He was a short, thin, brown skinned young man with a head shaped like a cashew nut. Mikies and Jesse played basketball at the campus courts together and had developed a friendship. People called him "The Snake" because of the way he moved on the basketball court.

"Alright, Mikies, hold up." Jesse said. Jesse called him "Mikies" because his friend had three other brothers with the same name -- Mikie Jr., Mikie Steve, and Mikie Joe.

"So what's up, Mikies? What you doin' over here at this time of the morning?" Mikies' squinted eyes were glassy, resembling two brown plastic footballs bobbing playfully in puddles of milk.

"Jesse, bad news, man. Bad, bad news." Jesse prepared his entire body for an unknown jolt.

"So what's up, man? This bet' not be no joke, I know you."

"It's Jimmy, man," Mikies said, his voice full of despair.

"What's up with him?"

"He was in a car accident late last night. A drunk driver ran a red light and broadsided him on the driver's side."

"Oh my God. He was just over here at around 9:30 last night wantin' me to go out partying with him," Jesse said.

"That's something!" Mikies said.

"Well, have you been to the hospital to see how he's doin'? Is he in intensive care or the emergency room?"

Mikie looked him square in the eye with an acute seriousness. "He ain't in no hospital, man. He's dead!"

Jesse's entire body moved as if he had just been thrown a professional punch.

"I can't believe it. I can't believe it!" Jesse said and then started crying, at first uncontrollably, but then slowly subsiding. The news left his mind in a state of complete disorientation. He kept turning it over and twisting it, and it kept coming up convoluted.

Mikies was unsure of what to say as the tears rolled down his face. He thought of Jimmy's promise of youth, his sense of humor, his way around the truth. Jimmy was an imperfect man, but a good one. He was blessed with a sincerity that went beyond definition. He possessed a renowned brashness that became his signature.

Jesse knew that he needed to get to chemistry class, as much as he regretted it. For now, all his eyes could do was focus on the sky. He was trying desperately to make sense of the senselessness of human frailty. His concern: What did eternity hold for Jimmy?

Jesse's eyes were focused south, but something provoked him to shift to the east. At that point, he noticed the gray clouds starting to move. The lukewarm rain was slowly starting to subside. Suddenly, amidst the sun bursting through the clouds, a brilliant rainbow appeared in sheer magnificence.

A feeling of confirmation came over him in a powerful way. His sorrow took flight. His joy had been renewed. He knew then that his message to Jimmy had been received. All he could do was whisper, "Thank you, Jesus!"

Mikies put his hand to his mouth to clear his throat. There was some nervousness in his voice. He said, "Hey Jesse, I'll check you out later."

"Alright then, Mikies, later on." As he clinched his fists tightly, he knew that victory was his.

Chapter 10

The next morning, Rose awoke at the same time as her father. Her movements seemed disconnected because she wasn't accustomed to seeing that hour. Her mother was not yet awake.

Her father asked, "What you doin' up so early for?"

"I wanted to talk you, Dad."

"What you want to talk about, Rose?"

"I want to talk about you, Dad. I want to know what makes you tick, your likes, dislikes. You know, for-real stuff." Sudden dread started to set in on Rufus like suffocation. He felt like an escaped convict who finds himself surrounded on every angle with such fear of death that breathing becomes more dangerous than not breathing.

Rose found her salvation in a couple of spoonfuls of Corn Flakes.

"So what's goin' on, Rose? What's on your mind for real?" Rufus asked.

"You are. I told you. Vivian used to be my friend," she said.

"What you talking 'bout?"

"I know all about everything between you and her and the baby too!"

"You got something all backwards, Rose," he said.

"Oh no I don't. I'm right on target."

"Don't get smart with me now, Rose. I ain't havin it."

"I'm not tryin' to be smart, Dad. I'm just letting you know that I know." Beads of sweat had protruded on Rufus's forehead.

"Rose, let's just drop that subject for now. This ain't the time or place."

In a tone devoid of all sarcasm, cynicism, malice and anger, she asked in a clear voice, "Well, if not now, then when?"

Rufus never felt more lost within himself. He never felt so much self-betrayal. He never felt so undone from being outdone. He stared into his cup of coffee with a bewilderment.

"So you're not denying that this happened?" Rose continued.

"It's something that I really don't want to talk about right now."

"All right."

Rose felt that she already knew the truth. She was just looking for an admission of guilt. As bad as she felt, she knew that her father needed to face the mean reality of knowing his fall. An equation had been turned and twisted. It would come up again, but silence would suffice for now. In minutes, Della was awake.

"Mornin', Mom."

"Good morning. What you doin' up so early?"

"Just wanted to talk to Dad a little bit," Rose said.

"About what?" Della asked.

"Just things," Rose said.

"What things?" Della asked.

"Nothing important, Mom, really."

"All right, I'ma leave it alone then," Della said with irritation.

Rufus was hidden out of sign in the living room, but listened to the conversation. When the conversation ended, he quietly went out the door to go to work. When the door closed, Della hollered out, "Rufus, is that you?" But he was too far gone to respond.

Nervousness began to afflict Rose. "Well, Mom, I need to get to school. Have a good day," Rose said.

"Yeah, you too." A gnawing suspicion was at work within Della. She didn't want to feel this way from her own family, but she had the feeling something was being concealed from her. She could not deny the fact that her instincts had pulled her coat, but she became overwhelmed with the idea that if she couldn't believe her own family, everything else in life was an untruth.

She wasn't going to let it ruin her day though. She knew that in due time, it would be dealt with. Slowly she walked towards the stove to get hot water for her coffee. She had already sprinkled one and a half teaspoons of Folgers Instant into the bottom of the eggshell colored porcelain cup.

Della walked into the dining room and turned on the radio to the early morning gospel program. James Cleveland was pouring out his heart singing *Precious Memories.*

Precious Memories, how they linger.

How they ever --- touch my soul!

She slowly sat down in her chair and languished in the innocence of the early morning hours. Every now and then that suspected mystery would try to creep into her mind like a cat that scratches at an aluminum screen door. Della immersed herself in a prayer of thanksgiving. The Clara Ward Singers moved peace onto her spirit, a peace that was almost sullen, yet full of power.

After the Clara Ward Singers, there was a brief intermission for commercials. Within moments, Mahalia Jackson came back with *Precious Lord, Take My Hand.* The song moved Della so greatly that it caused tears to flow down her face unwittingly. The entire room became filled with an anointing and a power that had true purpose. Her mind became bathed in the solace of time. Her joy had been achieved. A quietness had taken over.

Suddenly, as if from Satan, a loud, crashing, screeching noise filled the air. The sound was frightening and close. The enormity of it brought Della to her feet. She went to the window to find out what had happened. The noise was coming from only two houses down.

A crowd had gathered of mostly housewives in robes, bandanas and old house shoes. An altercation had been caused by a 79-year old white man named Norman Crawford who lived five blocks away. Crawford was a retired mail carrier who was on his way to the grocery store to pick up milk, bread and prune juice. Out of nowhere, a sharp, overwhelming pain in his chest had overtaken him. His breathing became difficult as piercing pains shot up his left arm. He hollered in anguish. Before he realized what was going on, his mint green 1964 Buick Special had lost control, jumped the curb and had headed in the direction of the Dickerson home.

He lost consciousness, but all of the strength contained in his right foot stayed on the accelerator.

The car smashed through the front of the house, leaving in its wake, glass, aluminum, wood, nuts, bolts, screws, and shattered cement. It went into the living room, tearing up the beige carpet, the lamps, a velour wing back chair, then came to a halt when it hit the plastic-covered loveseat.

Luckily, Mrs. Dickerson was upstairs when the car hit. When she came downstairs, she screamed uncontrollably at the sight of the mishap. Her alarm was not as much out of seeing her living room, but from seeing Mr. Crawford bleeding from the top of his head, as his body was dumped over the steering column. The cracked section of the windshield where his head made impact resembled that of an intricate spider web.

Della watched in despair as the paramedics retrieved the body from the vehicle and brought it out of the house. "Blanche, I'm so sorry, but I'm thankful that you didn't get hurt. That's a real blessing," Della said.

Della glanced down and saw feces running down Blanche Dickerson's left leg. Della put her arms around Blanche and took her down to her house to clean her up. Blanche spent the greater part of her day with Della. With her own power and strength, Della tried to help make her feel like herself again.

Della knew what she had been through and this incident added to the injury. For all intents and purposes, Blanche Dickerson was a woman acquainted with grief. It hadn't even been four years since she had attended the closed-casket funeral of her son.

Melvin was a twenty-two year old, wiry young man who had only spent nine months of anguish in the heated, tragic jungles of Vietnam. He had stepped on a land mine that had blown off his right foot. The impact lifted him six feet into the air 18 feet back against a tree.

His seargent almost threw up as he looked at his face and skull that had been severely lacerated from the branch of a tree. Melvin's neck had been broken, his left eyeball was gone, and his upper vertebrae had been shattered. The medics worked on him for twenty minutes, still amazed that he could survive the impact. However, the internal bleeding was so profound that death was a welcomed traveler.

It had only been 13 months since another incident threw Blanche into a season of agony. It involved her husband, Ezekiel "Zeke' Dickerson, a family-oriented, hardworking Christian man who always went to work on time and always paid his bills with the same zeal. Zeke was a man who eschewed evil and walked upright amongst his kindred. He worked as an elementary school janitor for 23 years. He stood 5'9" and weighed 210 pounds, and for 52, was in good shape.

One morning, Blanche cooked him a breakfast of scrambled eggs, Canadian bacon, grits and coffee. After twenty minutes, Zeke took two antacid tablets to ease the discomfort of indigestion. Relief came. No more thought was given to his aggravation.

Around 11:45, he was called to the school cafeteria to clean up a tray spilled by a careless second grader. Before he could even make his first swipe of the mop, a feeling of molten lava shot through his chest. Sweat poured down his face like condensation on the side of a sterling silver challis filled with ice water. He felt as if he was choking. Before the teachers could reach him, he fell over dead on the lunch table in front of sixty-three screaming, crying, second- and third-grade children.

It was without a doubt that Della had to continue to be there for Blance. Their two sons played together as children. Both of them went off to the same war as young men. The only difference was that one returned from death and the other one met an untimely end.

Chapter 11

Della called Blanche's insurance adjuster for her. Blanche appeared lost, as she stared away into unknown spaces. Twenty minutes elapsed into eternity. Blanche's sister, Lucille, arrived to take Blanche home with her. She would let her stay as long as she needed to until order could be restored. Lucille led Blanche out of the room by the arm. Blanche's hair stood on end, uncombed, unkempt, with her ends dried out and damaged. When Blanche left, Della called the hospital to check on Larry's condition.

She washed her hands with vigor, looking at how the soap turned into lather as she rubbed it against her hands. She began to prepare salmon patties, corn and green beans for dinner. The Kool-Aid had already been prepared, its sweetness causing a lightness in the brain.

The door opened and Rose entered with determination and quickness.

Della searched for solace in her cooking. She asked, "What you doin' home so early, girl?"

"There was a gas leak, Momma. It started with a few kids getting' sick. They all had the same symptoms. The principal and one of the janitors smelled gas so strong that it just about knocked them out. That's when they evacuated the building." She hesitated long enough to place her books on the walnut dining room table. "Who tore up Mrs. Dickerson's house like that?"

"An old man had a heart attack, lost control and ran into her house. Mrs. Dickerson was shook up pretty bad, but she'll be alright. She's at her sister's house right now."

"Her insurance company should help her get everything back together, right?" Rose asked.

"They should, hopefully."

Reality was more tragic. Reality was cruel. The reality was that after Zeke died, the insurance company raised their rates without warning. Blanche struggled, did all that she knew to do to make the payments. A month before the accident, Blanche's stove went bad. She had to pay to have some elements replaced. There was no money left for the insurance payment. She called and asked for 10 day grace period, but they refused. A letter explaining the cancellation of her policy was sent the same day. The policy had been in effect for 25 years.

"Mom, you look like you're worried about something. What is it?"

"I don't want to go into it, Rose." An unspoken force was causing Della's heart to fill with pain.

"Somethin' smells pretty good, Mom."

"Thanks."

When Rufus finally walked in, he was draped in weariness. "Della," he said. She ignored him.

"Della!" he called again.

She turned her head towards him with the swiftness of a tiger, rolled her eyes at him, and then said, "What do you want, Rufus?"

His mouth flew open in shock. "You seem to be upset about something, Della. What's botherin' you?"

"I can't put my finger on it, but something just ain't right."

"Ain't right with what?"

"Like I said, I don't know," she said, with her head kept focused towards the floor.

Rose stood there in a state of bewilderment. In silence, Della fixed Rufus a plate. As they sat down to eat, few words were spoken.

Slowly, the evening flowed into night. The television news reported on Vietnam, Washington, China and the Middle East. Della lay in bed with her eyes closed. She stared upward in the darkness.

Eventually, she dozed off, but her sleep was restless. She felt drowsy the next morning and lay back down after everyone had left. The brief nap helped to invigorate her and she caught a second wind.

She was motivated enough to clean out some of the dressers and closets in the bedroom. She began by refolding the bed linen. She then straightened out the underwear, lingerie, T-shirts and socks. She then found a perfume scented letter at the bottom of the middle drawer. Its contents were provocative and sensual. Della was shocked. The letter had been signed "your sweetheart, Vivian." A numbness came over her. Her stomach turned bitter from the hurt. Her face had a look that surpassed common grief. Her head pounded.

Della shook her head in shame and disgust as she continued to stare unwittingly at the words in the letter. At seven minutes before noon, she left to go to the hospital to check on Larry. She talked to him briefly and returned home to prepare supper. Her level of anticipation was high, but it crashed when Rufus didn't arrive at his expected time. He'd gone to the hospital after work to see Larry.

"Where you been, Rufus?" Della asked.

"I been at the hospital, Della, I'm sorry, I knew I shoulda called. I just wanted to see for myself how Larry was doin' today."

"I should call him up and ask him myself if you were up there." Her statement jolted Rufus.

"What're you talking 'bout, Della? Where did all that come from?"

"Never mind, Rufus. Whatever you do, that's your business. But you know what's done in the dark will come to light."

"Yeah, I know that. But what's makin' you say all this?" Della slowly grasped a foothold on her composure and tried not to let her emotions encompass her better judgment.

"Don't worry about it, Rufus. We'll talk about it after dinner."

"Yeah, that's fine," he said. Not a word was spoken during the meal. The emotions that danced in their eyes screamed anger. The rage, the doubt, mystery and uncertainty spoke volumes.

"So Rufus, let me ask you something," Della said with calculation and assurance.

"What's that, Della?"

The Rose from Sharon

"Have you always been faithful to me? I mean, you would never cheat on me, right?"

"Oh my God. What makes you ask me that?" His eyes bucked with surprise.

"Oh, I don't know. Curiosity."

"Yeah, but what makes you curious?"

"You don't need to worry about that. Just answer yes or no Rufus. How hard is that to do?"

"Come on, Della." His nervousness gave way to an answer unspoken.

"Yes or No?" Della said emphatically.

"What?"

"Yes or No!" she said again.

"No, then" he said.

"Are you absolutely sure? I mean I know they had those rumors swirling years ago about you having some half and half child out there, but you swore up and down that it was a lie. I couldn't say, because I never saw the child. All I know is what they were saying in the streets."

"Well, you know you can't believe none of that. People lie so much, Della."

"Yeah, I know that, but four or five people ain't gonna tell the same lie." Rufus became stupefied with silence.

"Why you questioning me like this?"

"Tell you what, hold on for a minute and I'll show you why," she said.

"So, you wanna explain this, Rufus?" Rufus sat there silent, not knowing what to say - not knowing what to do.

"So who is Vivian?" Rufus snickered in order to try and offset his uneasiness.

"So this is funny to you, huh?" Della stood there with her hands on her hips. Her anger was about to get away from her.

"No it's not funny, Della."

"Well, tell me who Vivian is then, Rufus. I ain't got all night," she said, irritation growing by the minute. "And before you start, please tell the truth," she begged.

"I ain't really got a whole lot to say."

"So now you ain't got nothing to say. Well, I know you had to have been goin' with this woman or screwin' her or something!"

Rufus continued his silence, since he had not yet arrived at the perfect lie.

"Why can't you just admit it! I already know you did it. I already know!!" Della shouted.

"How you know that?"

"Come on now, Rufus."

During this period, Rufus continued to speak boldly even though his stomach quivered with uneasiness. "Listen, I'm innocent until proven guilty."

Della lost her temper and the thought of reaching for a knife swiftly crossed her mind before she came back to her true self. "Nigger, yo' ass is guilty as sin!!!" Rufus continued to sit there, taking in deep breaths as sweat poured down his face. Della continued to stand over him hollering and blaming.

"Since you don't wanna tell me about it and you insist on sitting up here and lying to me, why don't you get you someplace else to stay tonight!"

"Come on, Della."

"Come on, my ass. I told you I ain't gonna let you make no fool outta me and I meant that!"

"Come on, Della, be reasonable."

"No you didn't say be reasonable, did you?" She went for a butcher knife and chased him out the back door, hollering, "Now you get yo ass out and you stay out!!"

"Alright, Della," he said, moving swiftly.

By this point Della was crying and asking him, "How, Rufus, how in the hell could you do this to me?!!"

Rufus just kept on walking with his head down, already filled with guilt. There was no beauty nor dignity in it, just feelings of regret, shame, embarassment. Although his heart was contrite, it would never be able to touch what had been inflicted upon Della. Her last words, before he moved out of earshot were, "You don't belong here anymore if you can't be honest with me."

The words stung. He felt a sense of loss. They had tunneled in far enough to prick him in his heart. They left him feeling undistinguished and simply undone. It was as if God had turned a spigot of lightning to full blast.

Rufus found a cheap room for the night so that his body could at least attain a semblance of rest for the next day. But that rest would not reattach the brokenness that had occurred within his spirit. His heart ached. All he longed for was the simplicity of life -- a cold Rolling Rock beer and some of B.B. King's blues to help give kinship to his troubles. When daybreak came, he had hardly slept.

The workday dragged itself slowly to its end. The blue of the sky, which was meant to soothe, brought only sorrow. As he looked at the green grass outside of the factory, it transfixed him. He found a pay telephone and called Della.

"What are you doin' callin' me? I don't wanna talk to you, Rufus." Her tone caused his intestines to churn.

"I just wanted to see how things were goin', that's all. I'm not trying to cause no trouble," he said, as if pleading for mercy from a merciless demi-god.

"Yeah, you've done enough of that."

"So I guess that means that I'm not welcome back home, huh?"

"That's exactly what it means," she said. Her eyes bucked with anger.

'Can I at least stop and pick up some clothes?" he asked with humility.

"No you can't come up in here. I'll put your clothes out on the porch if you want 'em." She hung up before he could say another word. The receiver clanged so hard, his ears rang. He twitched his mouth in irritation.

When he arrived, he found his clothes, shoes and underwear thrown into a bundle, sitting on the porch. After seeing how she did his clothing, he didn't waste time going into the house. He knew that at the time, his anger would have only provoked a more maddening argument.

"Damn it, damn it, damn it," he said as he sorted through the pile. He took a seat in one of the chairs on the porch, exhausted in his spirit and mind, hoping that it might quell the seizing anger on the inside.

"After all I've done for her, how dare she do this to me?" He leaned his head back in order to relax, but before he could ponder the situation, he was asleep. The rays of the sun bathed his arms in warmth as they sat on the armrests. In the dream, it seemed as if his subconscious was imitating some realm of life.

In his dream, he was dressed in a tuxedo, with a bouquet of roses in his hand. As he opened the front door of his house, Della greeted him with a kiss and a hug. She wore a beautiful full-length gown with elaborate floral embroidery on the side and front. She smiled as Rufus presented her with the roses. "I'm glad everything is alright between us now, Della."

"Rufus, you don't have to worry about telling me the rest of the story. It really don't even matter anymore," she said, smiling with raw savvy, her full breasts seething with excitement. Without warning, she pulled a small caliber revolver from her bra and pulled the trigger. The bullet entered his chest. Rufus screamed himself out of the nap, as beads of sweat poured down the side of his face. He gathered up his clothes, threw them into the trunk of his work car and went to the bank to make a withdrawal. It was a joint account and when he looked at the balance, he noticed that it was three hundred dollars less than before. He didn't even see the sense in confronting his wife about it. He just left it as it was.

He left the bank saying to himself,

"The Lord is my shepherd I shall not want. He maketh me to lie down in green pastures; He leadeth me beside the still water. He restoreth my soul. He leadeth me in the paths of righteousness for His name's sake. Yea, though I walk through the valley of the shadow of death, I will fear no evil for thou art with me. Thy rod and thy staff comfort me. Thou preparest a table before me in the presence of mine enemies. Thou annointest my head with oil. My cup runneth over. Surely goodness and mercy shall follow me all the days of my life and I will dwell in the house of the Lord forever."

Within minutes he passed a car that resembled Vivian's. That's all that it took to strangle his concentration. Thoughts of her instantly began to flood his mind in the way that water floods the streets of Venice. He stopped in at Big Lou's Café for a Pepsi-Cola. He felt that if he could only experience the exuberance of having that cold,

The Rose from Sharon

crisp dark brown cola going slowly down the back of his throat, then all would be close to normal again. As he entered, the heavy voice of a large woman boomed out over the back of the bar.

"Hey, what can I do you out of, Deacon?"

It was the proprietor, Big Lou. She was a woman who stood almost six feet tall and weighed 280 pounds. She had enormous thighs that rubbed together and would chafe whenever she failed to apply enough lotion to them. She had a heavy mustache that she refused to cut or trim.

"Big Lou, how you doin'? It's been a long time," Rufus said.

"I'm doing good. How about yourself?"

"I'm doin' alright, I guess. It's just me and the old lady are havin' some troubles these days."

"Sorry to hear that," Big Lou said, as she lowered her voice and spoke with concern.

"Yeah, it ain't been so easy lately, but I'm going to get through it," he said.

"I know you will, Deac. You're a fighter, a survivor. You don't let things get the best of you," she said.

"Yeah, I keep telling myself that."

"You going to be alright, Deac, I just know you are. Here, have this Pepsi on the house," she said, as her large hands gave him an open bottle over the counter.

They had both been acquainted with the tragic heartache. Rufus remembered when

Big Lou, short for Louise Stevens, was always bigger than all the rest of the girls. She also seemed to lack a certain grace that goes along with womanhood. There was a time when her insecurities made her unsure of her own sexuality. Because of her size, some people had already tried to define her with an unsuitable label. Those same ones fell under the assumption that she even married her husband in order to bring silence to her critics. In their eyes, it was more of a matter of trying to divert an entire mindset, rather than a matter of love. Her size also caused others to think that she was older that what she really was. Even at the age of 18, she looked 25.

Two months prior to her 19th birthday, 39-year-old Wilbur Matthews asked for and received Big Lou's parents' permission for her hand in marriage. They never viewed her early marriage as a blessing, but they did see it as being less of a strain on the overall household. They still had five children at home that made it a constant struggle just to keep a decent meal on their dingy dinner table. Mr. Stevens' meager salary as a janitor at both the police station and the Board of Education made the task of meeting ends a never-ending challenge.

Although Big Lou was a large girl, she was still sensual in many ways. As much as she fought it, all too often her mind would daydream about firm, young hips, swelled breasts and smooth female skin. As much as she denied it, the very absence of an Adam's Apple made her feel comfortable, unthreatened and somehow secure.

Big Lou thought that by marrying this older man, it would arrest her guilt. The true fact was that many of their views were as polarized as sun is from rain. There wasn't much that she did that pleased him, except some of the dishes that she, on occasion, cooked. Her frustration far outweighed his in every aspect of their relationship. Talks would lead to arguments that led to fewer talks. She started to confide in her friends even more. At times she was convinced that this was her only link to normalcy.

In fact, after she gave birth to their son, Wilbur Jr., the intensity of it all took on a life of its own. It left Big Lou trapped, fearful and forever mindful of her trauma. Wilbur's abuse had escalated into the vicious use of belts, broken bottles, work boots or whatever else might be handy to throw at the time.

Then Big Lou met a woman in church by the name of Norma Tisdale. She was a big-boned, handsome woman with an insatiable, aggressive nature. She had a fearless look in her eyes that shrunk Wilbur into a child. He felt threatened by her. It wasn't as much intimidation that he felt, but more that his self-appointed control over Big Lou was at stake. He'd watch when they talked and how Big Lou would hang onto every word that Norma said. Big Lou listened to her with intensity as if the very mysteries of the world and the deepest enigmas life were contained in the words that she espoused.

After awhile, Norma's visits to their home became more frequent and Big Lou's level of attention towards her was heightened. Norma

The Rose from Sharon

didn't even speak to Wilbur when she entered the house. Norma developed a genius at making Wilbur feel misplaced. There was a power that she had over Big Lou that he could not come close to. It was the way she looked into her eyes, along with a gentle touch.

Norma was only 26 years old, but was already twice divorced and the mother of a ten year-old son and a four-year-old daughter. One day when Wilbur walked in, he caught Norma caressing the left side of Big Lou's face. It startled Big Lou but didn't phase Norma in the least. Wilbur stood there, not knowing how to react, but Norma knew how to. "What the hell you starin' at, man? If you would treat her a little better, she wouldn't be upset all the time."

"What the hell you talking 'bout? I tell you what, bitch, you just go on and get the hell out of my house!!" Wilbur yelled.

"Nigger, make me get!" Norma yelled back.

But just as Wilbur was starting to approach her, Big Lou quickly stepped in the middle of them and said to Wilbur, "Leave her alone or else I'm leavin'!"

Norma's stare pierced clean through him. "All right. I see how this is goin'. I'm just going to leave you alone then, Norma. But you bet' not ever come back up in here or I'm callin' the police and reporting trespassing."

"No you won't, unless you want to go to jail yourself. All the times you done put yo' hands on me. I'll make sure they put yo' ass underneath the jail!" Big Lou said with determination.

"Oh, so ya'll going to go and double team ol' Wilbur, huh? That's alright. Ain't neither one of ya'll worth me getting in trouble for."

"That's right, come to yo' senses, man," Norma said.

"What I'll do is just file for divorce, tell the judge that you're an unfit mother and take our son myself," he said.

At that Big Lou went into a rage, charging at Wilbur with all that she had. Norma had to use all of her strength to restrain her.

"I'll kill you dead if you try to take my baby!!!" Big Lou hollered with tears flowing down her cheeks.

"Get ahold of yo'self, girl. This fool ain't even worth it!" Norma said.

"Let her go!" Wilbur hollered. "Forget ya'll, I'm going out for a drink." He left in a fury.

"Good riddance!" Norma hollered at his back. "Girl, leave him alone. Right now ain't the time," she said.

"What you talking bout?"

"Just trust what I'm telling you. Now ain't the time. Now stop cryin and get yourself together." Norma slowly moved her powerful five-foot, six-inch frame toward Big Lou and passionately hugged her and whispered in her ear, "It's going to be alright."

Big Lou had become enamored with Norma. She began to allow her to dominate every aspect of her life. Norma's visits were becoming less frequent, but that didn't matter because her influence was more intense now. When she would stop by, Wilbur disdained the very appearance even more than he ever had.

"So what is it now? You listen to her more than you listen to me." Wilbur said every time Norma would leave. When he said this, Big Lou would never respond. "Well, you just keep on bein' smart and you'll see what happens," he said.

"Oh, so you threatnin' me now?" "Big Lou asked.

"Take it anyway you want." Her fear of him had subsided. Her boldness had found its own voice.

****

Norma looked Big Lou in the eyes. She smiled and pealed out a laugh that shook the room. "Yeah, I figured that he was still botherin' you. Well, I'm going to put an end to it real soon." Big Lou looked at her with the wonder of a child.

"Just what are you talkin' 'bout, Norma?" she asked, her voice tinged with fear. Norma

laughed again. Her expression turned deadly.

"What you think I'm talking 'bout? He's got to go. Then once he's outta the way, we can be together without his interference."

"Come on, Norma, you can't do that." But with the mixture of cocaine and barbiturates coursing through her bloodstream, she only heard silence.

"I'm going to do whatever the hell I want to do and ain't nobody going to stop me!" Norma said.

"But Norma, it ain't got to come to all that. I mean, I'll just leave him and be done with it."

Norma stepped to her nose to nose and shouted directly into her nervous face, "Bitch, are you crazy! This man ain't going to let you leave him!"

"What you mean, Norma?" A change built up in Norma's light brown eyes.

"What is wrong with you, Big Lou? Trust me. I can look in his eyes and tell that he'll sooner put you in your grave before he sees you leave him." Big Lou breathed in order to try to control her tears. She used a Kleenex to pat at the tears. Her eyelids had turned red.

"He don't love you. He's just tryin' to control you to make you think that he loves you," Norma went on. "I know what I'm talking about, because I saw men down in Memphis who acted just like him. All they try to do is run some kind of game." Big Lou wanted to believe, really believe. She was confused by all that had been said. After all that he done, she kept thinking that things were going to get better.

"Believe me, things ain't going to get better. They going to get even worse than they are now." Norma said.

"Ya think so?" Big Lou said, while still patting away her tears.

"I know so. Besides, I'm the one who really loves you."

"Big Lou, now I got to know if you really love me back!" Big Lou stood quietly, but then Norma asked her again.

"Do you love me, Big Lou?" She looked her in the eye without flinching and without answering. Norma asked her a third time.

"Big Lou, do you love me?"

"Yes. Yes, I love you. I never loved anyone like this ever before" she said.

"You got to know that I'm really concerned, because I'm about to put my life on the line for you," Norma said.

The plan would be believable because Big Lou still had scars from when Wilbur had hit her just a week before. On a Wednesday, Big Lou took great pains in preparing Wilbur's favorite meal: liver, smothered in onions, with collared greens and mashed potatoes on the side. The meal was topped off with strawberry Kool-Aid and a slice of sweet potato pie.

What confounded him was the fact that Big Lou was overly

cordial to him. That behavior went against the grain of late.

"Did you get enough, Wilbur? I can get you more if you want." He couldn't remember the last time she had cared enough to ask him anything of that nature.

"No thanks, I'm pretty full." Wilbur stood only 5'8" and weighed 132 pounds, yet always had room for seconds, sometimes even thirds.

"I'm glad you enjoyed it," Big Lou said.

"Yeah, I damn sure did."

Wilbur looked at her and noticed that the nipples of her breasts were more alert than normal. There was an exotic excitement moving through her searching for a house of rest.

"Hey Wilbur, you want to have a little fun and play a game with me?"

"What you talking 'bout, Big Lou?

"I'll tell you what I want to do. I want to blindfold you and tie you up and play a game I call 'Smell This'."

"Where'd you come up with that?" he asked.

"I just made it up. The way it works is, I'll tie you up and you try to guess what it is I put under your nose."

"You must be crazy! No telling what you might try and put under my nose."

"It'll be fun, Wilbur. Come on, I'll give you some later," she said.

"Promise."

"Of course I promise." Wilbur was speechless. His feet began to move out of excitement.

"Alright, but his better be fun. You bet' not be runnin' no games on me," he said.

"So you're gonna play, baby?" Her voice was childlike. Not immature, just adventurous.

"Yeah, I'll go on and play."

"It'll be a game you'll never forget," she said with a sly seductive smile, as she caressed his chest.

"Girl, what you up to?"

"Nothin' but fun, baby. Nothin' but fun."

"Yeah, but you ain't been tryin' to have no fun. Why now?"

The Rose from Sharon

"I don't know, I just feel like it right now," she said.

"Alright."

Big Lou used rope to tie his hands and feet. She initially didn't use great force. Gradually she tightened the rope, ensuing no escape. 'Why you got to use a heavy rope like this to tie me up with? You tryin' to kill me or something?"

"Of course not, but this makes it more fun when it's more real."

"I'ma trust you this time," he said.

"You're in good hands, Wilbur." She put the blindfold over his eyes. "You're all set now, baby."

There were micro sized beads of sweat forming on the Wilbur's temples from his apparent nervousness. Big Lou was uneasy herself, but was striving to make it somehow subside. She retrieved a white carnation and placed it under his nose.

"That's easy. That's a flower, girl." She grabbed a bottle of vinegar that she had him smell. His head jutted back like a young buck. The tartness irritated his membranes. "Damn it, what the hell you tryin' to do?" he said.

"Nothin', nothin'. It's all part of the game," she said, as she snickered quietly to herself. She was in control. She then put a bottle of honey underneath his nose.

"I'd like some of that right now. That smelled pretty good."

"It's time for intermission now, Wilbur." She went over to the record player and turned on the 8-track. She put in a tape of Les McCann's and Eddie Harrison's *Swiss Movement* and played the song *Compared to What*. She turned the volume up as high as she could. The beat was insatiable, the voice of McCann, savage and raw.

Wilbur shouted, "Hey, turn that down. You going to bust my eardrums." Once the music hit full swing, that was Norma's cue to come through the back door. Violence reflected in her eyes. She lined up the baseball bat carefully with his head, pulling back and taking two practice swings. Then she swung with all the strength within her. The solid wood of the bat met the back of his skull with ferocious force. The wood cracked.

When the bat hit him, he let out a terrible holler as he fell to the floor, still tied tightly to the chair. The music drowned out the hollering as he whimpered on the floor draped in the mantle of his pain. The music was unable to purify the blood that flew across the kitchen. A small droplet fell into Norma's right eye. Norma stopped momentarily to try and wipe it, but that only made it worse. She noticed that he continued to squirm, so she hit him again with the same fierceness on the side of his temple.

During it all, Big Lou stayed in the dining room out of fear and guilt. One thing Norma took tremendous pride in was her reputed high threshold for pain. For this, she hid a six-inch needle under her skin. She kept it sanitized with rubbing alcohol. She pulled the needle out and as Wilbur lay on the kitchen floor amidst a sea of his own blood, she went to work. She rammed the needle all the way through his left nostril until it hemorrhaged his brain. He died right there on his kitchen floor that had not been mopped in two weeks.

When Big Lou came in and looked at that sea of blood surrounding Wilbur's head like a halo, she began to scream uncontrollably. Norma reached out to her, being careful not to get blood on her.

Their sentences were a light five years because their lawyer was able to convince the judge that the killing was in self-defense. What crushed Big Lou was that when they were released, Norma didn't even tell her she was leaving her for another woman that she met on the inside. It rattled Big Lou into a zone of distress, but after awhile, she saw her way to recovery.

Big Lou mastered the art of rebounding and in time, she was able to get a loan. At that, a life-long dream of owning her own store was realized. She had been acquainted with her own pain, so when she saw the melancholy look behind Rufus's eyes, a kinship linked them. She knew that beyond all the weight, there was still a daylight.

"Whatever got you down, Deac, believe me, you can get over it. Trust me."

"I know you're right, Big Lou, but you just don't know. You just don't know," Rufus said while rubbing his forehead, accentuating the minor wrinkles.

"Oh yeah, one thing I do know is that it ain't worth you mumblin' 'round here with your face long. It ain't worth you actin' like you lost your best friend."

The Rose from Sharon

"I know you ain't lyin', Big Lou, but you bein' kind of tough on me right now."

Big Lou snickered and replied, "Somebody needs to be tough on you. Man, don't you know that the Lawd could call you home anytime? He could call you home by the end of the day. Why cheat yourself by feelin' miserable? Life is too short for that and you already know it."

Rufus sat there and sighed. His nostrils flared in and out. He couldn't help contemplating the urgency of his present state. "Well, maybe he sent me in here just to see you. I think I needed to hear what you're sayin'."

"Right on, right on, Deac. Sometimes the strongest medicine is the best medicine. Sometimes, if it don't hurt you, it ain't going to help you, 'cause you never learn nothin' livin' in a rose garden," she said.

"I hear ya, Big Lou."

"I mean, people who've had a cushion all their lives and then all of a sudden they run into something hard and they're not equipped to handle it."

"You right, Big Lou".

"I seen it, man, when I was in the joint. You could always tell the ones who been livin' on a cushion all their lives. Something go wrong and they just fall to pieces. They be ready to lose their minds, 'cause they think that life ain't nothing but sugar and cream. Man, you know better than I do, Deac, that life ain't no sugar and cream," she said.

Rufus didn't say a word. He simply looked into the valleys of her eyes and listened to her.

"I ain't religious or nothing like that but I do know something 'bout the story of Job. He had everything but Satan put him to the test and he ended up losing everything. In spite of it all, he never lost his mind. He never lost his love for God. That is right, ain't it, Deac?"

"You preachin' now!" Rufus said.

"But not only that, because Job didn't lose his cool. When the test was over God gave him back more than he ever had!"

"That's so true, Big Lou," he said. Her words pumped blood into him. His weight remained, but something on the inside reaffirmed that he would survive. "I just came in for a Pepsi, but I've gotten so much more."

"You never know what life's going to throw at you. Believe me, I know, Deac. I had to grow up fast and quick. My family was poor, which kind of led to me leavin' the house in the first place. You know all about my marriage and all that other mess. I done been through some things and sometimes I wasn't sure whether I was going to make it or not. I knew that there was something on the inside that wouldn't let me give up and turn around. I wasn't about to give up for nothing and nobody!" Big Lou halted long enough to take a drag on her lukewarm beer.

"You going to be, alright, Deac. Just keep the faith, keep the faith. Remember, you always going to get more than what you bargained for when you come into 'Big Lou's Place'," she said.

"Yeah, but you just don't know, I've really screwed things up pretty good at home," Rufus said, with an uncharacteristic heaviness permeating his voice.

"Come on, man. Who ain't screwed up? Hell, you know I been in the joint. I've screwed up. Everybody's screwed up sometime or another. You need to stop feeling so sorry for yourself. You still da' man in my book," she said.

"Thank you." A knawing silence came between them in the way that a butcher's blade separates the chicken breast from the shoulder. Soon his bottle of soda was finished. He sat there, entranced by the swirls grooved in the glass. He looked at it as if staring into a mirror that contained the underpinnings of his soul. He needed to grasp for mercy.

"Hey, Big Lou, I'm going to take off now, but thanks for everything. I feel better leaving than I did coming in. What you said meant a lot to me."

She smiled and said, "Anytime, anytime, Deac. If you need me I'm just a holler away."

"Thanks Big Lou." He then slowly walked towards the door, as if in a funeral procession. As he set out to walk, the night fell upon him with a crushing vengeance. He felt as if he needed to ask permission to even look up at the stars. Their beauty was something that caused awe. Yet he wondered how he could stand before the all-encompassing power of a merciful God.

As he continued to move within his self-reflection, a star captured his attention. He was captivated to the extent that he challenged himself to see if he could remain focused on that star while he continued to walk. As he periodically glanced to the sky, he was aware that this was not the only beautiful star, but his challenge was to remain focused on that particular one. There was something about its individual beauty that seemed to transcend the logic of understanding. The strength of the others should have caused him to deviate, but he needed to prove to himself that he would stay with this "chosen one."

Slowly, a stream of clouds came across the midnight sky and then gradually faded from view. The star had disappeared. He found himself standing in his own front yard. A heavy sigh expelled from his lungs. He stood there and studied the intricacies of his home. He started to listen carefully, as it was his mind that brought his soul in for questioning. How did it all come down to this?

The weight of the day filled him. The sweetness of sleep was calling him like the mind-altering ecstasy that comes from unrestrained passion. He began to wobble from the weariness. He sat in his favorite chair on the porch. Within minutes, he was sound asleep.

The morning overcame him like the trauma that a crowbar causes as it strikes the brain and detaches the skull from its original form. He tried the front door knob, but it was locked. He then knocked and Della came to the door to let him in. "What you doin' here?" she asked.

"I just came to get some clean clothes and to wash up and then I'll be outta your way if that's what you want."

"Man, I can't believe you've got the nerve to even try to come back here."

"Della, I had to get something to wear and I needed to wash up. You got to be reasonable."

For the next three nights he slept outside of the house. The fourth night played havoc on his psyche. He was given time to put into perspective that which was real and negate his feelings of anger and hostility.

Della began to doubt her decision. There were dilemmas that languished in her mind as she contemplated the future. She didn't want to admit it, but her days took on a sense of emptiness. She wasn't necessarily lonely, but felt incomplete.

By now Rufus was staying with friends, and Della was in search for answers that the universe itself seemed to be hiding. She wanted to make sense out of the senselessness, but it wouldn't approach her. The felt nervous and uncertain. She needed answers, some form of mental reassurance that all would one day be well. She had progressed to drinking a pot of coffee each day, but she would still nod off through the entire day.

On a particularly sunny Tuesday, two weeks after Rufus had left, she received a phone call. It was a voice from her past.

"Della?"

"Yes," she answered.

"I guess you wouldn't remember me. It's been so long, huh?" the voice said.

"I'm afraid you're right, but I'm sure you'll tell me who you are, huh?" She tried vehemently to sprint through her memory just who this voice belonged to.

"How about David Anderson? Do remember a David Anderson?" She paused, striving to reinstate her memory.

"Oh my God!!! How you doin'? I haven't heard from you since high school!" she said.

"Yeah, I know, I know. So how have you been, Della?"

"Oh, I've had better days. Right now I'm havin' a few problems, but that's life. I don't even really feel like goin' into it."

"I don't mind, really," he said.

"Maybe some other time. Why don't you tell me what you've been up to?" she asked.

Right after high school, David did a year-and-a-half stint in 'Nam. He got out and went to work for Dow Chemical in Midland, Michigan. He worked there and went to college at night, receiving his bachelors degree in business administration and eventually accepting a job in management.

"That's really nice. I see you've done pretty good."

After he went into management, the company offered to pay for his Master's degree in business if he chose to pursue it, which he did. Two years after he completed his degree, they offered him a position as district manager for the southwest region of the country.

"That is really good."

"I appreciate that. I was happy about the promotion and the job, but there was downside to it all as well."

"What was that?" she asked.

"I was doing a great deal of traveling, which was part of the job. One day I came home early from a business seminar in Wisconsin. I wanted to surprise my wife so I didn't even call. As I began to walk up the stairs, I heard things I didn't want to hear. I opened the door and my wife was in bed with her second cousin."

"Oh my God, David, I'm sorry," she said.

He found a bat and started beating her and her cousin while they were still butt naked. They both ended up having to go to the hospital.

"You know, she always complained about me working too much and staying away from the house so often. But everything that I did was for her and the kids," he said.

"So you do have kids?"

"Yeah, two boys, David Jr. and Samuel."

"So, are you still married?"

"No, I've been divorced for five years now. We really tried to work it out and she was sorry for what she had done, but I had heard a few other things about her and my trust was just gone," he said.

"Your boys stay with you?"

"Naw, they're with their mother."

"So to what do I owe this call after all these years, David?"

He took great care in clearing his throat. "I'm going to be in the area in a few days and I thought maybe I could take you and your husband out for dinner. I don't see any harm with old friends catching up."

"I agree that there's no harm in it, but how did you know I was married?"

"Your phone number is in your husband's name and I ran into

Jack Wilson a few years ago in Las Vegas. You remember him, don't you? He ran track, went to Penn State?"

"Yeah," she said.

"He told me you were married to Rufus."

"It's a small world," Della said thoughtfully.

"So how's Rufus doin'?"

"I guess he's alright. He's not here right now."

"Where's he at? When will he be back?"

"I really don't know, David. I don't like talking 'bout it, but we're kind of split up."

"What do you mean, kinda split up?" he asked.

Della said, "We're not together, David. I don't really know how else to put it."

"I'm sorry, I'm sorry. I didn't mean to upset you. You really sound upset."

"I apologize for that. I didn't mean to get upset with you, but it's just been a little crazy. I hope you can understand that."

"Of course. I hope things can be worked out between you two."

"Time will tell," she said.

"I'm truly sorry, Della. Since that is the case, maybe we can make it for some other time."

At that, there came a pause, as she refused to give an answer. She diverted her attention away from the comment at hand.

"You never told me where you lived, David."

"Houston."

"Houston, Texas?" she asked

"Yes."

"That's a big place, isn't it?"

"Yes it is and it's getting' bigger by the day," he said.

"That's good."

"Well, Sharon is still just ol' Sharon. Not much has changed."

"That's too bad," he said.

"Where you stayin' at when you got here?"

"The Hampton Inn."

"In Youngstown?" she asked.

"Yes."

"That's a nice place. We've driven by there before."

The Rose from Sharon

"So, what is it Della? It's a definite NO for dinner, huh?"

"I'm afraid so, David. It's just not a good time right now."

"That's completely understandable. Not a problem. You have a good night, Della."

"Yeah, you too, David. Thanks for calling. It was good to hear your voice." She finally found safety in hanging up the phone.

In the meantime, Rufus needed to find out where he was with Della. When he tried to call her to talk, there was a callousness that permeated through the line that caused him to rethink. She admitted to forgiving him, but neither her demeanor nor tone coincided with her words. The bitterness lingered.

As for Della, she couldn't sleep after receiving that phone call. The morning came and she found herself looking up the number to the Hampton Inn. She asked the receptionist for David's room number, although she knew that he would not arrive until the next day.

"415, Ma'am."

"Thank you."

"He's not scheduled to check in until tomorrow though, Ma'am."

"Yes, I am aware of that," she said.

The next day she waited until 2:00 pm before she made the call. The phone rang twice before a voice was on the other end.

"Hampton Inn, may I help you?"

"Yes, can you give me room 415?" she asked.

"Yes, just a minute and I will connect you."

"Thanks."

"Hello."

"Hello, David, how are you? How was the trip?"

"It went fine Della, and how are you?"

"I'm fine, thanks. I just wanted to call and see how you are and to tell you I'm still interested in dinner, if it's alright with you."

"Why sure. But I thought you said..."

"Yeah, I know what I said, but I've had a change of heart. There's no harm in that is it?"

"No, no not at all. I'm just a little surprised, pleasantly surprised, of course."

"It would be good to see you again," she said.

"Yeah, likewise. But I must ask, what made you change your mind?"

"I honestly don't know, other than it just felt right. I mean, I thought about it and it just felt like the right thing to do."

"That's good Della. What about your husband? I'm a little concerned about that situation. My opinion may not count for much, but I just feel that maybe you should talk it over with him before you do anything."

"David, I wouldn't even know where to begin to look for him so that I could talk things over with him. He did some things in our marriage that he certainly didn't take the time out to talk to me about."

"I'm really sorry to hear that Della, but two wrongs don't make a right."

"So now you're saying that me going out to dinner with you is wrong?"

"No, not necessarily. I just don't want anything to be misread or misinterpreted."

"What do you mean, David?"

"All I'm saying is I wouldn't want you to be going to dinner for the wrong reasons. I wouldn't want you to do it in order to prove a point or to be vindictive or anything of that nature. That's all I'm saying."

"Naw, I'm not trying to do that. I don't need to do something like that to get back at him. If I wanted to do that I could think of a lot worse things to do other than that."

"I'm sure you could. I just know that men are funny about their wives being in the presence of other men without them being there with them."

"That's understandable," Della said.

"So, I will see you tomorrow night, right Della?"

"Yes."

"You have a good day," he said.

"You too." Guilt tried to invade her heart and mind, but she fought it off. She picked up the phone on three separate occasions in order to call and cancel the engagement, but didn't do it. She decided to go but to keep it as brief as possible.

The drive was uneventful. There was no hint of inclement weather, but there was a chill in the air. Della worked at convincing herself that "he's just a friend. There's no harm in having dinner with an old friend."

She found it hard to not think about her husband as thoughts of him threaded through her mind. The road was becoming a blur. She had no other recourse but to pull over and wipe away tears. As she pulled over, the tears came uncontrollably. She felt the only right thing to do was turn around.

Della sat in her car surveying the greenness of the fields, in awe of the power of God. A loneliness enveloped her which she had not known for quite some time. She became overwhelmed with the need to be understood. After a mental debate, she started back on her trip to Youngstown. All the while, she continued to question why she was going. Was it to recapture the magic of youth? Her hope was that it would be made manifest once she arrived.

When she did finally arrive at the hotel, uncertainty coursed through her as she pulled into the parking lot. She searched within herself for a sign that she was doing the right thing. As she walked towards the hotel her steps were calculated and her palms damp with perspiration. Anxiety visited her and caused her head to throb viciously. The expansive circular driveway impressed her. The perimeter of the driveway was wonderfully draped with red, white and canary-yellow perennials. The glass doors were tinted with the color of smoke and the immense adjoining sheets of glass seemed to have been constructed without flaw.

As she walked through the door, she noticed the foyer was finished in fine beige marble. The carpet was a dark tan with a short nap. The plants that sat against the walls were an aloe deviation, with spiny-toothed leaves. Their appearance brought forth a calm to her mind, of which she was sorely in need.

The odor of chlorine from the pool on the other side of the enormous room tickled her nose. She reached the entrance of the hotel dining room. There she noticed halophyte flowers sitting beside both doors. A short, olive-skinned man greeted her with a half-smile.

"How are you this evening, Madam?" he asked.

"I'm fine."

"Will this be dining for one?"

"No, I'm having diner with Mr. Andrews. David Andrews."

"I will take you to his table then."

"Thank you," she said.

Della followed closely behind him as he navigated through the crowd with the cold calculation of a cobra. "There you are, Ma'am. I will send a waiter to your table in a few minutes."

Tightly wound, she sat nervously, wondering where David might be. Shortly thereafter, he emerged from the men's room. She turned to her right as she heard her name called.

"Della!"

"Oh my God, David. You really look good."

"You too," he said, while hugging her.

She was impressed by the fact that his skin was still as taut as it was in high school. His

Afro was well-groomed, long on top, short on the sides. He stood six feet two and weighed 215 pounds. He was dressed in a Hart, Schaffner and Marx pin-stripe gray, wool blend suit. His teeth were flawless, his smile, remarkable.

"Girl, it's been so long," he said.

"I know, I know," she said.

"Have a seat, Della."

"All right."

"So, I told you quite a bit about me over the phone, Della. Now why don't you tell me about you now?" he asked.

"Ain't a whole lot to tell, David. I mean I've been a housewife with two children. Boring stuff, right?"

'Wrong. Being a wife and a mother, you hold a very important key to the greatness of society. Let's face it, raising children is one of the most difficult jobs to have."

"You've got a good point there."

"Your kids still home?"

"My daughter is, but my son is...well, he's kind of at home too."

"All right," he said.

"My daughter writes for the school newspaper and my boy sells cars. Buicks. But he's in the hospital right now because of a car accident."

"That's too bad."

"It was serious. He could have been killed," she said.

"What caused the accident?" he asked.

"Bad brakes they said, but the police suspect foul play." David didn't comment, but merely waited for her next statement.

"Just thinking about it really gets to me."

"Do you think your son has enemies out there?"

"I don't know and don't want to think about it. Who wants to think that kind of stuff about their kids? But I can't act like nothin's wrong because somebody shot at my daughter awhile back while she was standing in his room holding a baby that she was watching for a friend," she went on.

"Obviously your son has had some dealings with people who play for keeps," he said.

"I've been thinking that same way, but I guess I just haven't been able to accept that."

Finally their server appeared. She was a tall, dark-haired woman with penetrating hazel-brown eyes and a smile that was pleasant, but indifferent. "Good evening. My name is Sheila and I'll be your waitress this evening. Are you ready to order or do you need a little more time to decide?"

"If you could just five us a few more minutes, we should be able to decide," David said.

"Yes, Sir."

Minutes later the orders were taken and the menus gathered. David slid his chair back just far enough to cross his legs for the sake of comfort. Della noticed that something wasn't altogether right. His gray argyle socks failed to hide his entire ankle. It was the skin tone that caused her uneasiness. The tone of his face, hands and neck were substantially darker. Even the texture failed to have the same cohesion. It finally dawned on her that it was a prosthesis.

David giggled lightly to himself as he said, "It happened in 'Nam, Della." An embarrassed quiver shook her bottom lip.

"You look nervous. Don't be. To be honest with you, I think I get around better than some people who don't have to have this," he said.

"I had no idea," Della said, trying not to look as startled as she felt.

"Come on now. How were you supposed to know? I don't publicize the fact that I have a prosthetic leg, but I'm not out looking for sympathy either. I was in a deep, deep depression for three months right after it happened. Then I began to realize how foolish and wasteful pity parties are. I mean, they really are, when you think about it, because, after all, everyone has problems. Why waste time dwelling on problems when we all should spend more time coming up with solutions?" He paused for only a moment, "After all, Della, life is too short as it is."

"I just feel a little, stupid, that's all," Della said. She started to bite her lip.

"This is what 'Nam did to me."

"I'm sorry," she said.

"It happened awhile back. Over time, you just learn to accept it. I can't do anything about it." For the moment, dining became unimportant.

"It's only gone from the ankle down. I guess what makes me feel better and grateful is the fact that I at least still have a leg. What's even more important is that I'm still alive. I saw a lot of death over there. Believe it or not, I feel guilty for making it when so many others did not."

"David, you can't beat yourself up for comin' back alive. It's a blessing that you did. I believe that it was God's will that you came back, so there's nothing to feel guilty for," she said.

"Oh believe me, I am grateful to be alive. After talking to some other guys who came back to the world after the war, they feel that same guilt."

"I've heard how bad it was," Della said.

"I don't like talking about it too much, but it was like living in Hell. You couldn't even go to the bathroom in the same place, because the enemy was always looking for lifestyle patterns. If you ate in the same place, showered in the same place or whatever, you would certainly be an easy target."

"Lawd have mercy. That's terrible."

"The certainty of death is ever present, while the uncertainty of life completely envelopes you." Before his sentence was completed the waitress had returned with their food. Della looked and noticed the distance and hurt in his eyes.

"Are you alright, David?" she asked.

"Yes, I'm fine. I was just thinking about things that I need to forget."

"Oh, I see."

"Well, the food looks good. I'll say grace so that we can eat," he said.

"All right."

They both bowed their heads. "Heavenly Father, thank you for this food we are about to receive. Let it be nourishment for our bodies. Now Lord, I also ask that you bless Della and her family in a special way. All these things we ask in your Son's name. Amen."

"Amen," Della said.

"Let's eat, Della."

"I want to thank you for including me and my family in your prayer."

"You're welcome."

"How's it taste, Della?"

"It's delicious."

The evening ended and confusion laid waste. Her act of impulse gave small remedy. It lent to her no balm for healing. The evening enchanted her, while her conscience, at the same time, scolded her. Her mind pushed its way back and recoiled itself around all of the uncertainty that was Rufus.

She knew that his flesh became her flesh, that his blood somehow through divine provocation, had been joined with hers. Therefore, the pain of him polluting and contaminating their flesh with an uninvited soul was overwhelming. The sadness of it reverberated, robbing her of sleep. She took counsel as to what to do about Rufus.

As she headed towards home, she drove with steadfastness. Suddenly, bright lights glared into her rearview mirror. A black Camaro swept around the side of her car. Her fear was overwhelming. Her breathing grew more pronounced and her heart beat like a V-8 engine in full throttle. The Camaro sped off, only to be stopped by a highway patrolman three miles ahead. The driver was arrested for driving under the influence of alcohol and driving with an expired license.

When she finally made it to bed, sleep was true consolation. It felt like the sweetest intoxication.

****

Rose was on the cusp of entering her junior year. She had been engaged in learning about the power of burning bridges and the strength of erecting new ones. She was in search for determination to see her through almost anything. In spite of her academic successes, the problems that visited her parents tore at her.

"I can't help it, Mom. I'm just mad at the things that Dad has done to you, to us," she said.

"I know," Della said.

"I really wanted this to be a good year for me and for all the family. I even been thinking about talking to the pastor about Daddy," Rose said. Della looked at her with an expression of disconcerted restraint.

"Ain't no need for that, Rose. That ain't gonna solve nothing at this point. I'm more upset than you are, but we got to try and be sensible. We still family."

"So you've forgiven him?"

"I'm praying to try and forgive your father. As much as this hurts me, I know it's the right thing to do. Also, this is family business and it needs to stay that way," Della said.

"You don't think people out in the streets aren't talking, Momma?"

"I'm sure they are, so why go on and make a bad situation even worse?"

"It don't make no sense to me," Rose said.

"So what is this? Now you're getting smart with me, Rose? As if I ain't got enough to worry about." Della tried to restrain herself but ended up slapping Rose on the right side of her jaw.

"Just what has gotten into you where you think you can talk to me any way you want to? You think you old enough to sass me now?" Rose held her cheek as the tears welled up in her eyes.

The Rose from Sharon

"No, Ma'am, I don't think I'm old enough to sass you. I'm really sorry, Momma. It's just everything that happened," Rose said between tears.

"I know a lot is goin' on, but we've got to be strong for ourselves and for one another. Your dad has hurt me in ways that you'll never know, but I know that God will get me through it. Right now, we can't turn on one another. We just have to trust that God will get us through this."

"Yes, Ma'am," Rose said.

"Rose, I'm sorry for hittin' you, but the last thing I need right now is to have you disrespect me."

In a voice steeped with deep contrition, Rose said, "You're right, Momma."

"You know, right now, I feel that I need to go check on Larry at the hospital," Della said.

"That sounds like a good idea, Momma."

When they arrived at the hospital and came to Larry's room, he was asleep. Even within the confines of his sleep, his face appeared to be contorted in pain. They noticed that his breathing was heavier than usual. They'd sat near the bed for a short from of time when one of the nurses came through the door.

"Hello," the nurse said.

"How are you?" Della asked.

"Just fine," the nurse answered in a voice saturated in arrogance.

"I'm Larry's mother, Della Johnson. I don't recall ever seeing you here. You must be new."

"My name is Nora Hughes and yes, I am new," the nurse said as they shook hands.

"Well, how is Larry doin'? He looks like he's in pain," Della said.

"He's not responding to the medication. I think the doctor is going to run more tests."

"Where is the doctor?" Della asked.

"Not in right now."

"Do you know when he will be in?"

"I'm not sure, Ma'am" the nurse said. Della began to notice a hint of aggravation in her voice. It felt almost as if the nurse was sending her a message that she didn't want to be bothered with her continued line of questioning.

"So you don't know why he's not responding to the medication?" Della asked.

"No, I don't know. But you can trust that we are doing everything within the best of our ability."

"I'm glad to hear that, but, I must confess that I'm very disappointed that my son hasn't made more progress."

"And I told you that he's not responding to the medication. He was given a blood transfusion earlier today and we thought it would strengthen him, but it hasn't." Della turned her head away while the nurse checked Larry's vitals. When the nurse completed her task, Della asked to speak with her outside in the hallway.

"Yes, Ma'am?" Nurse Hughes asked.

"I can't explain what I'm feeling, but it's not good. I don't want to say that I don't trust you or trust what you say, but I should be getting more answers than what I've gotten. My son is close to being unconscious right now and nobody seems to have any real answers."

"I'm sorry that you feel that way, I really am, but you have to believe that we really are doing the best that we can right now. I don't know why your son is not responding better than he is. All we can do is prescribe and medicate," Nurse Hughes said.

"What nursing school did you go to?"

"I don't really think that's any of your business. What's your reason for even asking me something like that?" Nurse Hughes said, as the volume in her voice became magnified.

"You need to watch who you're talking to, nurse." Rose came out into the hallway to try to diffuse her mother's anger.

"Momma, we in the hospital," she said.

"I know where we're at!"

"Mrs. Johnson, I have taken an oath to do all I can for the betterment of all patients."

"So when you say all people, that would include black people as well?" Della asked.

Nurse Hughes's anger was now apparent from the redness that

came into her face.

"That was out of line!" she said.

"No I'm not out of line! You are, because I can see that you're prejudiced. I can see you don't really care about your patients. Don't insult me telling me about oaths. What are your oaths supposed to mean to me? White folks been breakin' oaths to black folks ever since we been in this country. Now what makes you think that I should believe that y'all going to start keeping your word now?" Nurse Hughes was acting as if she was going to walk away from Della.

"Don't you dare try to walk away from me. All I've got left to say to you is that if my son doesn't get any better, you'll be explaining it to my lawyer."

"Have a good evening, Mrs. Johnson." Della declined to even reply to her words.

There were certain questions in her mind as she watched the nurse walk down the hallway and then turn left at the corner. Della had become more disturbed. She felt that this woman's demeanor didn't fit that of a nurse, for it seemed too sinister.

Within the channels of her own mind, she fought with the phenomenon of good and evil. She struggled with the idea of having to tell Rufus about the treatment that Larry was receiving. The reality in her heart told her that she didn't even want to speak to him. In fact, she had wrestled vigorously with the possibility of going to a lawyer to pursue a divorce. She had issues with confronting the finality of divorce. She hadn't even discussed it with her children. No doubt, it would be her choice, but they would be the casualties of the marital chasm that would be created.

Whenever she prayed, there was something in her prayers that was telling her no. She realized that she needed to call Rufus.

"Hello," Rufus said.

"Hello, Rufus."

"Della, I'm surprised to hear from you. How's it goin'?"

"Good, but I just called to talk to you about Larry. You know he's really not getting any better."

"It takes time, Della."

"No, no. There's something not right with his condition," she said.

"Well, what do you think is goin' on, Della?"

"I just got a feeling that something's goin' on at that hospital that they're not telling us about. I can't prove it. I just feel it. Also, one of the nurses that they have now, I mean, she made me so mad, I was about ready to kick her."

"Now hold up, Della," Rufus said.

"She just had a real bad attitude. I mean real bad."

"So what do you think they did, give him the wrong medication or what? They're only human," he said.

"I know they're human," she said.

"I also know that you wouldn't be sayin' this stuff if you weren't feelin' it," Rufus said.

"That's right, I wouldn't even be thinking this if I didn't have a reason to think somethin' was wrong," she said.

"I'm going to go up there and talk to his doctor and see if I can't get to the bottom of this," Rufus said.

"I know my imagination might be runnin' crazy, but who's to say that the same one who messed with his brakes might be payin' someone in the hospital to try to hurt him," Della said.

Once again a strange silence momentarily suffocated the life out of the conversation.

"I'm really getting mad, but, if what you're saying is true, we've got to move fast," he said.

"I'm going to try and call this specialist that the hospital has working on him and then I'll call you back," Della said.

"That sounds good. You do that."

Della dialed the number and allowed it to ring a dozen times. She then dialed the main number to the hospital operator, asking her to page the specialist. The operator reported that he was not in the facility, but upon his return, she would have him call her. She then called Rufus back. "The doctor wasn't in" she said.

"That's not good. We need to try to get him transferred to another hospital as soon as possible," Rufus said. Della met his comment with a heavy sigh, as well as a thick cloud of worry.

"This is crazy. It ain't even makin' nonsense. I'll tell you what.

The Rose from Sharon

I'm going to call the hospital administrator in the morning to see what they can do," she said.

"Let me know what's goin' on then."

"All right," Della said, as she quickly hung up the receiver.

Her sleep that night was like that of a storm. Mental anguish weighed heavily on her mind. She found herself wrestling out one nightmare after another. At the end of the night, she was finally able to sleep. She rose later than normal and Rose had already left for school.

Della again called the hospital. When the operator answered, Della said, "May I speak to the hospital administrator?"

"Just a minute before I transfer."

"Thank you."

When the call finally went through, the voice on the other end contained feminine authority as it responded with, "The hospital administrator's office. May I help you?"

"I would like to speak to the hospital administrator."

"What's it in regard to, Ma'am?"

"Transferring a patient."

"For what reason would the patient need to be transferred?"

"I'd like to talk to the administrator about that."

"I will transfer you."

"Thank you."

"Charles Lavender speaking," the voice said.

"Mr. Lavender, my name is Della Johnson. My son is a patient at your hospital and I would like to look into getting him transferred."

"Transferred to where? To another hospital? But why? What seems to be the problem?" he said.

"I just have some suspicions and concerns that my son is not receiving the best of care," she said.

"What leads you to feel that way?"

"Just a feeling that I have about a certain nurse."

"Have you discussed this with the doctor yet?"

"No."

"Well maybe you should do that first, before you make a decision."

"I can't seem to reach him."

"Our doctors are supposed to be reachable at all times in case of emergency. I'll tell you what. I'll reach him, discuss this matter, and give you a call back sometime today."

"That sounds just fine with me. I do appreciate it."

"You're welcome. I'll talk with you later," he said.

The wait went on. Time moved like an addled heart that's unsure of its next beat. It became an overwhelming, horrific anticipation. When she tried to call Charles Lavender again, she didn't get an answer. At that, her rage became momentous. She tried once again to call Mr. Lavender, but again, there was no answer.

The next morning, Della went to the hospital to see Nurse Hughes. "Listen, I'm not going to waste no time. I'm just going to tell you like it is. I want to have Larry transferred and I won't accept no excuses," Della said in an unflinching manner.

"There is no reason for your son to be transferred. He's getting the best treatment and he is in good hands," Nurse Hughes said.

"I don't believe that. You're full of it, lady."

"You should try to calm down, Mrs. Johnson, because the nursing staff here makes sure that Mr. Johnson is well taken care of. His recovery is simply taking a little longer than any of us expected."

"Why is that?" Della asked.

"The human body is a tricky machine, but it's also a very powerful one. We can't really say when this person or that person will recover, because everyone mends at a different rate."

"I know that. I'm just real suspicious of you people, especially you," Della said, as she gave her a dead-on look.

"I'm sorry to hear you say that, but you have to realize there has been some progress. Very little, but some. You simply have to be more patient," Nurse Hughes replied.

"What?! You gotta lot of nerve saying something like that to me, when the last time I looked at my son he looked like he was ready to die! You've really got a lot of nerve. You really do!"

"Just try to calm down and be patient."

"No. I want him moved and I want him moved now!"

"That's not possible. Your son is in no condition to be moved. If we moved your son, we would be putting his life in direct danger and we could be liable for that."

The Rose from Sharon

"I think his life's in danger now and I will still hold you liable, no matter that happens."

"I'm trying real hard to remain professional, but that statement was definitely out of line," Nurse Hughes said.

Della left the hospital felling out of kilter. She went to the cheap, one-bedroom flat where Rufus was staying. "We need to do something about Larry getting out of that hospital and we need to do it real soon," she said.

At first, Rufus didn't respond. His face, twisted slightly in deep thought. His hands were anxious. "What's wrong, the hospital's still not talking right?" he scratched his head.

"That's right," Della said, with her arms crossed.

"Let me think about what we need to do," Rufus said.

Accomplishing her goal to not tarry long, she headed towards the door while telling Rufus, "If you come up with something, give me a call."

"I will." As she left, Della's mind remained in a frame of utter disturbance. Her brow was wrinkled by worry. She went home and talked to Rose about her day at school and other small topics.

Within a few hours she sat down in order to watch the CBS Evening News with Walter Cronkite. At the end of the news broadcast, they ran a profile special. The profile had a brief, yet thoroughly effective look into the life of a brilliant young lawyer from Philadelphia who was running for the office of governor for the state of Pennsylvania. He stood six feet tall, and had a square jaw, sandy blond hair, a pencil-thin mustached, and piering blue eyes. His name was James Buchanan Porter, the son of a proud, steelworker father and a loving mother who typified the dutiful homemaker.

Della thought that he seemed like a fine young man, but she had grown accustomed not to trust any politician. Rose sensed a nervousness within her mother.

"Mom, you seem like you have something heavy on your mind. Do you want to talk about it?"

"Naw, I'm alright." Yet there was a startled look in her eyes.

"Are you sure?"

"I'm fine, Rose, but thanks for askin'," she said breathing in an unnatural rhythm. As the darkness of night quickly took the day captive, Della headed to bed. The sun came up the next morning and glistened on the cinnamon-colored leaves that were brave enough to go the distance against the dazzling strength of the wind's last dance.

Della needed to make her way to the hospital. Upon her arrival, she found Larry in a deep sleep. She sat down next to his bed, placed a light kiss on his cheek and quietly walked out of the room. She went home and put a load of whites in the washing machine. She then looked in the freezer to see whether any pork chops were left. There were two packs, which she took out to thaw.

She opened two cans of corn and two cans of green beans before she headed for the task of looking for mashed potatoes. There was no doubt that she could be done before Rose came home.

It was almost time for the news. She told herself that she's only watch a little of it because she wanted to get back to the hospital. There was a certain news story that just wouldn't let her walk away. The story gripped her. It was mainly about the tragic murders of several young men. The murders baffled the police because of the randomness of it all. None of them could be zeroed in on because they occurred throughout the entire nation.

There were two in Florida, one in Wyoming, one in Texas, two in Michigan, one in New York, two in Ohio, one in Utah, two in Georgia and four in Pennsylvania. The authorities had been unable to come up with a clear motive. Some of the victims had traffic records and a few had been arrested for marijuana possession. None of them had committed any crimes that seemed to warrant death. The victims had only two similarities: they were all close in age and they had all served in Vietnam during the same period of time.

Della made it to the hospital as soon as the newscast ended. Larry's expression was alert and his responses more keen than they had been in days past. "How you feelin'?" Della asked.

"Better than I was. For awhile there I felt like I didn't know what was gonna become of me," he said with a breathless sigh. "So how you doin', Momma?" he asked.

"Oh, alright I guess." But her expression told of a saga that ran counter to what she had spoken. "You know, Larry, I was watchin' the news before I came over, and well, I don't even know why I'm askin' because I know you wouldn't know him."

"Who?"

"Did you ever hear of a man named Jim Porter when you were over in Vietnam?"

The name rang in his ears like a thousand bells.

"Yeah, I knew him. He was my platoon leader, a sergeant. He was something else. I mean, really something else. He was very driven, very committed to what he believed in."

"You know he's running for governor," Della said.

"You're kidding!" He shouted more in amusement than disbelief.

"No. They just did a profile on the news about him."

"Oh yeah."

"There was a shot that they showed over in Vietnam and this guy in the picture looked a lot like you and that's why I wondered whether you knew him or not." Larry didn't respond.

"Yeah, Porter was really hard on us over in 'Nam, but it helped make us become one of the best platoons over there."

"He looks like he's on the ball, but he also looks suspicious," Della said.

"He did some crazy, crazy things. He was so driven that he wanted to win at all costs, even when all the odds were against him."

"What d'you mean by that?"

"It was so much madness goin' on over there. Some of it, I can't even mention, can't even talk about."

"I can just imagine. Lord have mercy, I'm glad you made it back alive," she said.

"Momma, most of it I don't wanna talk about or think about," he said.

"It's getting late, Larry. I'm gonna get back home so that you can get some rest." She bent over to gently plant a kiss on his forehead.

When she arrived back home, the phone was ringing. Rose quickly picked it up.

"You got home just in time, Mom. The phone is for you," she said.

"Hello?" Della said.

"Oh, how you doin'?"

"Yeah, I know I was supposed to call you back, but I had to go to the hospital to check on my son."

The voice on the other end asserted, "I can understand that, chile."

"Well, I'm not sure when I'll be able to have time for coffee. Hopefully soon," Della said.

"You just call me when you have the time so that we can discuss that business we need to discuss."

"It should be soon. In the meantime, you take care and have a good night," Della said, while slowly twisting a pencil between her right index finger and thumb.

"That was somebody I never heard call here before," Rose said.

"That was Mrs. Badeaux. She goes to the AME Church. She want me to work on a committee with her that combines both of our churches in a fundraising project.

"She talks a little different," Rose said.

"I guess to some people she might be a little different, but she's not from here. She's from Louisiana," Della said.

"Oh really?" Rose responded. There was a slight tilt of her head as she waited to hear more information.

"She's supposed to be a little different, because people say she has some kind of supernatural powers," Della said.

"What do you mean by that?"

"People didn't know what to think of her after she predicted that President Kennedy was gonna be killed two days before it happened. That really scared a lot of people. I had heard some strange things about her. Someone told me that when she was a little girl down in Louisiana, she danced around the dead body of her grandmother and the old woman came back to life."

"That's something," Rose said, standing there with legs and arms crossed.

"They even said that she had two husbands at the same time before she came up here," Della said.

"Oh really?"

"One husband happened to be fifteen years older than the other one. It was said that she put a spell on the older husband and he howled at the moon all night long like some kinda werewolf. And while he was doin' that, she'd be somewhere else with the younger husband in another room in the same house. The older one knew it all along, but he was so caught up he couldn't leave."

The rumors didn't stop at those few things. It was purported that she could look at chicken bones and make them chatter, make grown women squat and piss in the middle of the street in broad daylight, turn urine into ice water and make grown men slap their own mothers and call them everything but a child of God.

"Well, Momma, I'm gonna go to bed now."

"Alright then, Rose. You have a good night." Shortly thereafter, Della made her way towards her own bed.

The next morning, Larry took a drastic turn for the worse. Something sinister had been put into play overnight. Someone had injected the wrong blood type into his system, causing his blood to congeal. Oddly enough, Nurse Hughes was on watch that night. Luckily, the mistake was caught in time for it to be remedied. His life would be spared.

Without question, someone had developed an itchy trigger finger. The sinister sin took shape in its own revelation as Nurse Hughes promptly submitted a letter of resignation. The hospital tried calling her to see what happened, but her phone had already had been cut off. They even went as far as having the authorities go over to her house to investigate, but she had already left town without a trace.

Della was beside herself. She made dangerous vows as to what she would do if Hughes was ever found. Her heart thumped quickly. Her anger was causing a rise in her blood pressure. When she saw Rufus, her first words were, "I told you, didn't I? I told you something wasn't right about them people."

"Yeah you did. I just wanna know why somebody's after him." Rufus said, turning away in anger about the incident. A momentary silence stiffened the room.

"I think this thing is bigger than the hospital. Whoever's after him, if they didn't get him in the hospital, doesn't mean that they can't get to him at all," Della said.

"I want security around his door until he is released." Rufus said.

Within a day, the police station was able to have an officer on guard around the clock. The hospital was still unable to trace the whereabouts of Hughes. They did discover, however, that her real name was not Hughes, but Porter. The deeper coincidence was that she was the first cousin of Larry's old lieutenant, Jim Porter.

The mention of Porter to Larry triggered subconscious thoughts that made themselves apparent in his dreams. One October day, Larry watched with fear as he heard Porter shourt at his superior officer, Lewis Cunningham. Flashes of Satan were heard in his voice. "I'm tired of your bumbling ass. You're gonna get my platoon shot all to hell."

"You're gonna do what I say or else," Cunningham said.

"Or else what? Come on, this is the second time you ordered us just a hair away from direct enemy fire!" Porter said. He was now four inches away from Cunningham, face-to-face, eyeball-to-eyeball.

"The 'or else' is if you disobey my orders, I'm gonna have you court-marshaled," Cunningham said. Their argument ensued, while Porter's men took cover from certain enemy fire, bombs and explosives.

"I want you to say that again!"

"I said, if you disobey my orders, I'm gonna have your ass court-marshaled." Infuriated beyond restraint, Porter inhaled violently. He tried to gain a sense of composure. He thought he had prayed for an alternative. He mumbled something violently to himself and turned around to face Cunningham.

He spewed, "Why don't you *comprende'* this, Officer!"

He took out his pistol and shot Cunningham directly in the forehead. As he was falling backwards, Porter fired another round directly into his chest. His body fell over the cliff where they had just stood. Porter called the platoon together for an impromptu meeting. As they stood, listless in a sea of unfamiliar emotion, Porter began to speak. His men were open-mouthed with shock.

"Men, I know what you saw was disturbing, but you must understand that what I did had to be done for the survival and betterment of every one of you in this platoon. I did it because of my love and concern for you men. I did what I thought was best. Now

The Rose from Sharon

you know as well as I that if this were to get out to the higher-ups, they might not know just how to take it. In fact they would seek out the most severe form of punishment that they could possibly impose upon me. So, for those reasons, I command you men to not utter a single word to anyone about what you saw this evening. As far as you all are concerned, Cunningham was killed serving his country. It's as simple as that. I want you to see what happened this evening as purging the system."

The emotions of everyone in the platoons ran from stunned to infuriated to completely unnerved. But they all honored the solemn oath that they took. Many of them were unable to even give Porter the human respect of eye contact.

Larry woke from dream damp with sweat. As he slowly came back to himself, all he could say was, "Oh my God," over and over again. The clarity of his dream shocked him into a senseless reality. Within the fraction of a moment, Larry realized that Porter was out to get him.

Who had the answers that he now so desperately needed? Hope came in the form of a man named Sinclair Henson. He was a writer for the Cleveland Plain Dealer, but was also one who loved to investigate, in his spare time, stories which held strong possibilities for intrigue. Sinclair's cousin, Charles Henson, was in Vietnam and was very familiar with James Porter. In fact, he witnessed Porter torture one of his own men who had the audacity to challenge his authority. He witnessed Porter ordering his soldiers to kill innocent civilians in cold blood.

When Charles's cousin, Sinclair, caught wind that Porter was running for governor, his curiosity intensified. Charles knew many of the men in Porter's platoon, but he had no leads in how to reach them.

His intent was to have Sinclair set up interviews with these men, shed light into the allegations. He knew a story of this nature would illuminate his journalism career. It would also bear some light on Porter so that the citizens of Pennsylvania would be able to get an up-close and personal look at the man who would attempt to be king.

Sinclair put out ads in newspapers all over the country describing just who he was looking for. For two months, he had gotten no response from anyone. He was going to pull the ads, or at least put them in other places when the replies slowly started to come in.

These men had high anxiety bent on telling their stories. The mystery surrounding the deaths of those young men was becoming more apparent. Porter was hell-bent on power, and would stop at nothing, not even death, in order to become governor. In spite of a life with an abundance of flaws, Porter possessed an attribute that made him a true reader of the character of men. He knew the men who served under him much better than he revealed. He based most of his judgments on the three levels which human nature makes assessments: hatred, tolerance and devotion.

He knew the ones he could trust, the ones who he could trust some of the time, and the ones who would stab him in the back at a moment's notice. In truth, he didn't really trust anyone. Therefore, his mission would have to be to destroy all, leaving no voices from the past to speak in defense of truth.

His path of destruction was based on a grading system of sorts. The As were the ones he could trust. For these, he would let them suffer for awhile, delaying their deaths, playing with their lives as if it were his own to give or extinguish. In most of the cases, their form of death would be from poison, strangulation, or the wrong blood type being administered in a hospital room.

The AAs were the ones he could only partially trust. For these, the thing that he had prepared for them was a gradual cat and mouse game before some unforeseen accident would befall them. A boat would capsize; perhaps a stray bullet would fly from a police officer's gun.

AAAs were the backstabbers. Porter hated backstabbers with a passion, though one himself. No mercy was given to them. Many of these were handled by some of his Green Beret friends. Porter would have a story fabricated about them being flagrant drug fiends who had run up exorbitant drug bills. Sometimes the story would be that of a gambler who had lost control and found himself in a quandary. Porter had his people put the word out on the street that some were extortionists, thieves and hustlers.

He'd have drugs planted on them and then set them up for arrest by some of the corrupt cops that he bankrolled. These same cops would arrest them and when they saw that they were not being taken to a police station for arraignment, they were told they were only going to be talked to. In reality, they would be taken out to some quiet, barren location and shot in the back of the head, gangland-style.

In every circumstance, if the police found themselves being questioned, they would simply say that the victim had resisted arrest. Who would question the law?

What became more suspicious to Sinclair was the fact that some of the men he was set to interview were mysteriously dying. At that point, he had no real clear-cut evidence against Porter. In time, controversy had begun to swirl as to how Porter was able to amass such a large campaign fund. This led to an investigation and the authorities peering into his past in Vietnam.

Slowly, his power base was thwarted.

Three months before the election, Porter was arrested and forced out of the running. They were able to prove that his campaign money had been amassed through illegal means. Oddly, everything except the murder of Cunningham had been exposed. At his trial, he was found guilty of misappropriation of funds as well as for various war crimes. He was fined

$150,000 and sentenced to 20 years-to-life in a federal prison in Illinois. Larry felt the intervention of God on the day that Porter was sentenced.

At the same time, Rufus was finding that the burden of his guilt was becoming harder to live with. He began spitting up blood. His headaches became more severe. The struggle to sleep at night was a challenge that he was losing more and more frequently. These were indications of a wreakage in the spirit. He felt that, in time, something would have to give. The hour had come to hold court.

Every morning that he woke, it felt as if he had wrestled with Satan all night long. He would awake with the thought that said, "What if I don't make it to Heaven and the insanity of Hell is waiting for me?"

He longed for peace. He made up his mind to call the church that morning to set up a meeting to talk to the pastor. The meeting would take place at noon on the upcoming Saturday. His hope was that the pastor could shed light onto what he should do. He longed for an altar to lay his burden upon.

When Saturday arrived, it brought with it a warm sunrise. Rufus woke early and poured himself a bowl of Corn Flakes. He picked up the coffee pot and filled it with water. The radio broadcast the news and some Top 40s. Around 10:00 am, an insatiable desire came over him to call the pastor in to cancel the meeting.

The wrestling match had started again. A tug-of-war with consciousness was ensuing. The noon hour quickly approached and he arrived at the church with a knot in his stomach. As he entered through the blue tinted-glass doors, the pastor was there to meet him.

"How you doin', Deacon Johnson?"

"I'm fine, Pastor. How are you?"

"I'm fine, Sir. Let's go back into my office," he said. When they arrived, the pastor offered up prayer, asking for God's provision during the meeting. The pastor was stylishly dressed, wearing a navy blue sport coat with nautical styled brass buttons, gray flannel trousers, white shirt with a red and blue-striped tie and cordovan leather loafers.

He was 5'9" with a medium build. His face was chestnut brown with a scar over the left eye, a souvenir obtained in 1956. At that time, he was a young man given to stealing cars on the lower side of Pittsburgh. He received the cut from a sharp, bone-handled switchblade after an altercation he had one night when he was trying to steal a 1954 Pontiac Star Chief. He was blessed to be able to walk away with his life intact.

Six months after that experience, he found the Lord after attending a summer revival that one of his cousins had invited him to. He began serving the Lord from that night forward and didn't turn back.

"Now what did you need to discuss with me, Deacon?" There was a long space of what he felt was safe hesitation before he spoke.

"After doing a lot of soul searching and a lot of thinking and a whole lot of praying, I feel I need to make some decisions," Rufus said, nervously rubbing his hands across his blue jeans.

"And what might those be?"

The Rose from Sharon

"I feel that it's time for me to step down from being a deacon, until I can get some things resolved in my life."

"I'm not that surprised about that. I've been hearing things, and usually I can ignore it, but I've heard it too often. I don't really need to mention it, do I?"

"No you don't." Rufus's eyes tried not to show the void that his heart was feeling.

"I appreciate and respect your decision. It's made my job easier, because I was intending on approaching you about this."

"I don't really know what to say."

"So if I may ask, is it safe to assume that the allegations are true then?"

"Yes, they are." Rufus said quickly, not wanting to dwell long on any of the syllables.

"I'm really sorry to hear that. I know none of us are perfect and we all do things outside of the will of God. When you are in a position where other people are watching you, then you have to be that much more accountable for your actions. Also, being in your position, it brings a negative light upon the church, which cannot be accepted or tolerated."

"I understand, Pastor. This is why I'm making this decision. With all that's going on I haven't given God nowhere near what I should be giving him," Rufus said.

"No one's perfect. You know that. But have you asked God for forgiveness?" he said.

"Yes I have and I believe that I am forgiven."

"Well, if that's the case, you can't let Satan keep bringing up things that God has already forgiven you for."

"I agree with that and I also know that I can't keep sitting up here acting one way, when I'm not even able to focus on the Lord right now when I'm in church. I'm always thinking about all my other problems." A release of anxiety came about the more he talked.

"You've got to give them to the Lord and let Him fight your battles. That's the only way you're gonna get victory over this!"

"You're right again."

"Well, if this is something that you've settled with the Lord, then I certainly can't stand in the way of that," the pastor said.

"Thanks for understanding, Pastor."

"Not a problem. Now do you want to make an announcement tomorrow during morning services?"

"I can do that."

"I just want you to know that I'm behind you 100% and I'm very proud of you for facing your responsibility to yourself and to the church. You'll be a better man for it and God is really gonna bless you for it." At that, the pastor prayed with him, then said goodbye and Rufus then headed for the door. The rest of his day felt justified.

When the pastor ended his sermon and the invitation to join the church was being extended, Rufus rose from where he was sitting and took a seat on the mourner's bench. The eyes of many in the congregation were in a state of shock. Some of them sat there simply mouthing the words, "Oh my God." The choir sang, *Just as I Am*, an anthem full of melodic contriteness. Its theme spoke to the fact that one doesn't have to come to God with pretense or elaborate words.

When the song ended, the pastor walked over to Rufus and put his hand on his shoulder. He said, "Brothers and sister, Deacon Johnson has something that he'd like to say. Deacon Johnson, just say what's on your heart and remember your brothers and sisters are prayin' for you."

Rufus stood there with his soul laid bare before the entire congregation. He took his time as he began to speak. He inhaled deeply, as he said, "Good morning, everyone. There's just a little something I'd like to say to you all this morning."

At those words, he was met with a chorus of "We're prayin' for you, brother. Just let

God have His way."

"First of all, I want to confess Jesus Christ as my personal Savior and I want to thank Him for saving me and for lovin' me." He hesitated momentarily and then proceeded. "I just feel so humble this morning standin' before you all and I'm grateful that you all are prayin' for me."

A wave of "amens" rushed over. "This is really hard for me, but I just want to say that I haven't always done the right thing. I haven't done the right thing since I've been married and I haven't always done the right thing since I've been a deacon."

The congregation echoed in one voice. "Lawd have mercy."

"I don't think I need to go into any detail about what has happened. Some know, some don't know and some think they know. The real bottom line is that the Lord has forgiven me."

"Hallelujah, Hallelujah," the choir shouted and clapped.

"But, because there are some unresolved issues in my life..."

"Pray, church, pray," the pastor hollered out.

"...I feel that the time has come for me to step down from the deaconship. It's not permanent, but just for the time being, until I can get things resolved. Let me correct that comment, until the Lord resolves those things that need to be resolved." Della sat in the choir stand completely speechless.

"This is a decision that I have been in prayer about and one that I certainly feel led by the Lord to do."

Before the pastor spoke, he wiped the sweat off of his brow, the by-product of a fiery sermon. "Well, we can't argue with that, can we, church?" A smile came over the pastor's face. "Amen!"

"I just ask that you all continue to pray for me and I will certainly continue to pray for you."

"Amen! Amen! Amen!"

Well, according to those amens, brother, you can certainly count on the fact that you'll be in our prayers," the pastor said.

"Thank you, Pastor."

"Now, I don't want to hear about anyone bothering Deacon Johnson about what it is he needs to work out. That's between him and God. Your job, our job is to continue to pray for him and keep lovin' him."

He felt absolution.

As Rufus slowly walked back to his seat, the congregation met him with thunderous applause. He approached his seat and his fellow deacons stood up and one by one, hugged him, and told him that they loved him. Rufus did all that he could to fight back the tears, to no avail.

"The Lord was in this place today, wasn't he, church?"

"Yes, sir," they all hollered out, as if subservient children striving to please a loving parent.

"Let us now receive the benediction. Now unto Him who is able to keep you from falling and present us faultless before His throne with exceeding joy. To the only wise God, our Savior, be glory, majesty, dominion and power. Now, henceforth and forevermore, Amen!"

Della left out the side door without a word to Rufus. All that she could lend was a glance of indifference. On the other hand, Rose ran and gave her father a hug. "Daddy, I'm so proud of you, I don't know what to do. I'm glad you stopped ducking and dodging," she said.

"I do feel better. It's like a weight lifted off of me."

"I'm sure you do feel better."

"What you got planned after church, Rose?" he asked.

"I'm just goin' home to eat dinner and then watch some TV."

"After you finish eatin', stop over to my place. I want to talk to you."

"Alright, sir, I'll do that."

"I can pick you up if you want."

"No, I like to walk."

When Rufus reached his small apartment, for the first time, the mildewed smell of the building went undetected in his nostrils. As he removed his suit and found more relaxed clothing, the lightness carried on. He grasped the scent of restoration from God. All that he had the energy for was a bologna sandwich with marcelled potato chips and a 16-ounce bottle of Pepsi.

He straightened up a few items and then watched portions of what the television had to offer. By now he had hung up his navy blue suit. His hair was semi-combed. There was a brown ring around the neck of his white dress shirt. At five till three, there was an anxious knock on the door.

"Who is it?"

"It's me, Dad." Rose had changed into blue jeans and a Penn State sweat shirt.

"All right. Come on in," he said with exuberance. "How you doin, Rose?"

"I'm feeling pretty good right now, Dad," she said. Her freshly brushed smile was exuberant.

"I'm glad to hear that. Well, come on in and make yourself at home." She took the chair that was caddy corner to the sofa that he was sitting on.

"I'm really proud of what you did today, Dad. I could tell you were speaking from the heart," she said.

"There wasn't reason to speak any other way. I always taught you and your brother to be honest with others and to also be honest with yourselves. That's where it's at, because if you can't be honest with yourself, then you're just livin' a lie and that's just what I've been doin'. Life's too short for playin' games."

"That's true."

"So what's on your mind? What do you feel?"

"Honestly, I feel a lot of things. I really sometimes with you were back home with us and I wish Momma and you got along better. But I keep telling myself that it's all going to work out in time. I got faith." Silence momentarily penetrated the inner surface of the room.

"You're bein' positive. That's one good thing that you got from your dad," he said.

"I try to stay that way, Dad. There really isn't much reason to be anything other than that," she said.

"That's a good way of looking at things. I wonder about some of the same things you just mentioned, plus a whole lot more."

"Like what?" she asked.

"Life. Things, Rose. Your brother and you are on my mind quite a bit."

"We're doin' alright."

"Yeah. I know that. But a man, if he is any kind of man, wonders what kind of message he's going to leave behind as he gets older. I'm not a writer so I don't have a book to leave behind. I'm not an artist, so I don't have paintings and sculptures to leave behind. But I do have you guys, thank God. Y'all are my books and paintings, my legacy. All I'm tryin' to say to you is that I want to do everything that I can to leave behind good books to read."

"You've done alright, Dad."

"Naw, naw, I'm nowhere close to where I want or need to be. I know that you know about Ricky." Rose froze in her chair as the words made deep indentations on her mind. She ran beyond a zone of speechlessness. An unexpected heaviness took over. The power of the air became a symphony of uncertainty. It became surreal.

"I know you're surprised that I knew that and that's why you froze up the way that you did," he said. She sat there. She had been stunned to the bone. "Rose, I'm not ashamed of him. I'm ashamed of myself. I love him and even though it's been love at a distance, I love him just like I love the rest of y'all. I'm glad that you've gotten to know him."

"Yes, I am too, but why didn't you ever try to spend time with him or try to get to know him?" she asked, as she slowly sat back in the chair.

"I didn't want to hurt your mother nor you guys. Trust me, it was hard on me to keep a distance from him. I would see him as he walked to school. I would even meet his mother at certain places and give her money for him. I knew that if I tried to get close, then I would want him around me that much more and I knew, in time, that it would cause a problem. I never wanted to hurt anyone in any way."

"It makes since now. I understand a little better," she said.

"How's your writing coming along?"

"It's goin' alright."

"Have you thought about what you want to do after high school?"

"I'd like to go to college. I've been working hard to keep my grades up. I just hope the money's there when the time comes."

"That's good, that's good. I was hopin' you would make that choice. You know that I'm going to do everything that I can. What about what you're going to study?"

"I'm not real sure right now. If not journalism, then it'll probably be education or business."

"You can't go wrong with any of those choices." A dry, arid silence pervaded. "So when was the last time you saw Ricky?"

"I'm not real sure."

"Yeah, I understand, after all, it's been a lot goin' on in the family, plus school. There's only so many hours in the day, right?"

"That's right, Sir." Rufus's attention was balanced between a volumeless TV with the sound of the radio, which was only loud enough to hear certain melodies. He heard the mellifluous voice of Aaron Neville singing, *If - you - want - something to play with, go and find yourself a toy. Baby my time is too expensive and I'm not your little boy.*

There then came a smooth transition. The beat shifted. Neville continued to command each verse with sweet power, *If you - are serious. Don't play with my heart, it makes me furious. But, if you want me to love you, then baby, I will. Girl, you know that I will. Tell it like it is. I'm nothing to play with, go and find yourself a toy."*

The song was one of Rufus's favorites. Rose knew that because the song was played often in their home. She dare not speak a word until the songs' conclusion. Particular interest was given to the verse that stated, *Life is too short to have sorrow. You may be here today and gone tomorrow. You might as well get what you want. So go on and live, Girl go on and live. Tell it like it is."*

"Lawd have mercy, Rose. Now that's a song there. That man knows he really sang that song," he said.

"I know, Dad. That's one of your favorites. I remember when Momma and you played it at home all the time."

"I don't know what I was thinking. Do you want something to eat? I got some pop too if you want. I haven't cooked yet, but I can get you a sandwich or something together.

"No thanks, Dad. I'm alright." In her mind, there was an uncertainty as to just what her father wanted. She knew that small talk was not his forte. He had her over for a reason beyond what had apparently been spoken so far. She knew that whatever lay heavy on her father's mind, would bear down its weight on her heart. Rufus sat back for a minute and just closed his eyes. "If you're tired, I can go."

"No, no, I'm not tired at all. I'm just thinking, or as the smart people would say, reflecting." Rose sat back in preparation of what his next run on words would be. "Reflection, what's that word mean to you?" he asked.

"Let me think for a minute. Reflection is showing back to us a part of ourselves. You know, like the way a mirror shows an image of ourselves back to us," she said.

"That's deep. That's one way to reflect. But, to think about things is another way of reflecting too," he said.

"Yes, I know."

"I guess right now I'm feelin' both of those kinds of reflections. I'm thinking back on my life – what I could have changed and what I'd let stay the same. You ever think about that Rose?"

"Every now and then I do. I mean, I think everybody does."

"Well, one thing in life that I don't regret is having any of my children. I don't regret that one bit."

"I'm glad to hear that," she said.

"You know, I'm the first one to admit that I haven't always done the right thing. I'm not even going to use the 'human' excuse. But one thing I do know is that children are a gift from God and if it wasn't His will for a child to be born, then he wouldn't allow it. So everybody that's here is supposed to be here," Rufus said. His voice rose in volume and power.

"You're right, Dad."

"You see, Rose, God's been dealin' with me on this. Until lately, I been beatin' myself up for some of the things I've done. You know what they are so I won't spell 'em out. The main thing God has shown me is that 'His grace is sufficient'."

"That's good to know, Dad."

"The Apostle Paul prayed three times that God would take away the thorn in his flesh. But guess what, God didn't take it away. But he gave him the strength to endure whatever he had to go through. It seems to me like God was tryin' to teach Paul something. The reason I say that, Rose, is because after that, you never read about Paul complaining about anything else. That's because God had shown him that He could bring him through anything. All you gotta do is learn to trust Him."

There was no immediate response from Rose, but she had been ignited towards the strength or righteousness.

"That's how I feel right now, Rose. I know that God's grace is sufficient and I know that whatever I have to go through, He'll take me through it. No matter how big or small, no matter what the situation, I now believe I can go through it."

"That's good, Dad." Rufus walked to the sink to pour himself a glass of water.

The Rose from Sharon

"You did mention to your mother that you were comin' over here, didn't you?"

"Yes, sir." Rufus took a deep breath, then momentarily hesitated. He looked Rose in the eye with a look that, at one time, frightened her.

"Let's go see Ricky," he said. Rose's breath hesitated within her chest, like a stalled car or a frozen January morning.

"You want to see Ricky? Why?" she asked.

"It's very simple. I want to go and see him."

"I'm surprised to hear you say that. I was just wondering whether or not there was a certain reason for you wantin' to see him."

He smiled at her. "Does a man need a reason to go and see his son?" Amusement lingered in his voice.

"No sir, not at all. I'm ready to go whenever you are."

"Rose, I just can't let it keep on goin' like this. It's like I told you, I want to leave books behind. In order for me to do that, I've got to get to know this boy. I know he needs me and I certainly need him."

"You're right, Dad."

Chapter 12

Rufus did care about Ricky. It had gotten harder to talk around and pretend that he didn't. He had also cared about his mother.

She was a good woman caught up in a bad situation. The day she died in that hospital room, Rufus cried like a baby. She was sweet, but cursed with a life of suffering. Rufus came on the scene when she was at one of here many low points. She was vulnerable. He thought that talking to her and showing a little attention would make a difference. It did. It went further than it should have.

Rose looked at him quietly. She felt a combination of disgust, sympathy, and love, all tempered with the salt of confusion. Rufus stood stoicly, his mind reliving a history that drained him. He was thinking about the day that he found out Ricky's mother was pregnant.

For days, he hardly ate and his sleep was like a deprived animal seeking comfort. Neither one of them wanted this to happen. Their passion produced a fruit that they were not willing to deal with. Abortion was discussed. He gave her one hundred dollars to have it done. After that, he didn't speak to her for four months. The absence didn't remove the worm that twisted within him. One day, when she called the house, Della answered the phone. Ricky's mother pretended like she was one of the secretaries at work calling to ask Rufus for overtime. Rufus took the phone.

"How you doin'? Haven't heard from you in a while. I just wanted to tell you that I just couldn't go through with it."

The Rose from Sharon

"You're jokin', right?!"

"No. This is no joke. Try to be understanding. I'll talk to you later. Bye." He held the receiver to his ear for one full minute, allowing the deal tone to permeate his thinking. He had become so lightheaded, he wasn't sure of his capacity to keep standing.

"Let's get ready to go and see Ricky." Rose entered the car with caution.

"Today is the day," she said.

"You're right." Rufus drove noticeably slower than his usual speed. When they arrived, he pulled the car up to the curb in an unobtrusive manner. A quiet breeze pushed through the air. The leaves on the trees were somewhat overgrown. Rufus took a deep drag from the air hoping that it would lend him its life.

"I think I'm ready, Rose."

"You're more than ready and I'm very proud of you for doing this," she said. He went to the door and knocked briskly. There was no answer. He knocked the second time more vigorously.

This time the fragile voice of an old woman asked, "Who is it? Who is it at my door?" The voice was scraggly and full of the pain of living too many years.

"I'm Rufus, Rufus Johnson, Ma'am."

"Do I know you?" she asked.

"It's been some years. I don't know if you remember me or not."

"Well, what is it you want?"

"I'm here to see Ricky."

"Now what is it you want with Ricky?"

"I just needed to talk to him for a while, that's all."

Her voice became excited, nervous, as if it had received some exalted strength from on high. "But, but, but why? You some kind of police or something? Is he in some kind of trouble? Oh Lawd, Ricky's in trouble."

"No, Ma'am, no, no. He's not in any trouble. He hasn't done anything and no, I'm not a police officer. I'm just a friend who wants to visit with him."

"Now what was your name again?"

"Rufus. I just want to visit, Ma'am." His patience was fading, but his determination stood firm.

"I guess that's alright. Come on in." The old lady slowly opened the door. Her face was lined with the sorrow of many sunsets. Her memory of life's sweetness had been dulled to the point that death became more welcomed than another candle on her birthday cake. Her dress was a dingy pink with green, blue, and yellow plaid Her hair was the color of cotton.

As they entered, the pungent odor of the room dug a new tunnel into their nostrils. They fought a new fight just to head off turning their stomachs.

Rufus finally came back to his equilibrium. "How you doin'? It's good to see you," he said, extending his hand. Rose also extended her hand after her father's salutation. The old woman looked tired and full of despair. Rufus's eyes quickly scanned through the room. Ricky was sitting in a chair in the other room, engrossed in a television program.

"Hey Ricky, how you doin'?"

"Rose, Rose. Hi Rose. How you doin'?" His enthusiasm grew at the sight of her.

"So what you been up to, Ricky?"

"Nothin' much. After I go to school, I don't do nothing but come home, do my chores and watch TV. That's all, Rose."

"Well that's good, Ricky. There's nothing wrong with that."

"So who's this, Rose, your dad?"

"Yeah it is. He wanted to come over and meet you." At this point, his grandmother had made her way into the kitchen and began to stir the pot of soup beans that she had turned down to a simmer. She stood with one hand on her hip, studying the pot.

"Ricky, my name is Rufus Johnson. It's nice to meet you." Rufus gently shook his hand. Ricky said nothing. He simply stared at Rufus at what could have been described as amazement.

At that point, Rose and Rufus invited themselves to sit down.

"Would y'all like something to drink?" the grandmother hollered out in a weak voice from the kitchen.

"No thanks." Rufus said no to a beverage, although his throat was as dry as the Mohave. He didn't want to chance the dinginess of the glasses he saw sitting on the sink.

The Rose from Sharon

"So, what made you want to come see me?"

"You've been on my mind and I've just been wonderin' how you were doin'. I'm sorry I didn't call first, but I didn't have a number."

"It's just good to see ya', Rose."

After the old lady finished with the beans, she slowly went back into the living room and picked up the throw she was crocheting. She tried to ignore the conversation they were having in the dining room.

"How's school goin'?" Rose asked.

"It's good. We make stuff, practice our names and take trips to different places."

"That's good, but the real reason that I'm here is to talk to you about something really important."

A silent but heavy stream of frozen air moved through the room like a dangerous animal. For two perfect minutes, the sensation of it all made Rose's left temple thunder in nervousness.

"Ricky, try to brace yourself for what I'm about to tell you. The truth is that you and I are brother and sister, because this is your father."

'What! You playin' a joke, right?" His eyes shot open with excitement and disbelief.

"No Ricky, it's true. I know it might be hard to accept, but it is true. I wouldn't joke around about something like this." He stared at Rufus.

"Ricky, it's true. I am your father, and I apologize to you for just now letting you know this. But I have been keeping an eye on you. It's been hard on me also; much harder than anyone would ever understand."

"I can't believe it!" Ricky said. Tears began to well up in his eyes.

"Ricky, you don't have to cry. It's going to be alright, son." They both hugged tightly.

"Why couldn't you come to me sooner? I needed you," Ricky said as he wiped his tears away with the side of his hand. His right leg dragged.

"It's really hard to explain. All I can say is that I'm sorry. Try to accept my apologies." Ricky went to Rose to give her a hug.

"It's good to know. I just still don't understand why you're just now tryin' to get to know me."

"There are a lot of reasons. Believe it or not, I was scared of rejection. Scared of how you'd react, or what you might think or say. I didn't know whether it would even be a good idea to get attached to you back then."

"I don't even know what to say."

"Let me just say, Ricky, that I'm growin' up. I've been through some trials of my own and it's made me realize how important life is. It's made me not take things for granted like I once did. And it's made me value the things that matter, like my children."

"Okay."

"I figured, for me to really know what I'm all about, it would help me to get to know what you're all about." Rufus said.

"So you're trying to get to know me for your own good?"

"No, no, that's not what I meant. I need to get to know you for both of our good. You're a missing link in this life of mine and you've got every reason in the world to feel bitter, man, upset at me. I don't know, you might even hate me. You have to believe that God has been dealin' with me tryin' to make me a better man. I couldn't go on living with myself. I didn't want to live a lie anymore, actin' like you don't exist when I knew that my blood pumps through your veins!"

"Do you love me, though?" Ricky asked. Rufus became silent and deliberate, as he exhaled hard, not knowing what words to use to fill that moment.

"Yes. I do love you."

Suddenly, all three -- brother, sister and father -- hugged one another intensely. The old lady continued stirring in silence as she wiped the tears away from her cheeks.

"I want you to come and visit me anytime you want to, Ricky."

"Yes, sir."

"Well, see you later," Rufus said. "Goodbye, Ricky."

As Rufus prepared to open his driver's side door, he looked over the hood of his car and straight into his daughter's eyes. There was a determination there. "Now we need to go and pay your friend a visit."

The Rose from Sharon

"My friend who, Dad?"

"You know who."

"Oh, now I know."

"You do know where she lives, right?" Rufus asked, as he accelerated away from the curb.

"I know, but are you sure this is something that you want to do?"

"This is something that I have to do. I done put all this off long enough as it is." Rose couldn't form a response. She just gave directions to the destination.

"You see, Rose, when you come to the point where your mind is made up, you can't let anything or anybody get in your way."

"You're right," she said.

"On some things, you just have to stand firm." Rufus put his foot down on the accelerator.

"We'll get there, Dad."

"I don't mean to speed. I guess I'm just encouraged. It went better with Ricky than I thought it would. That makes me feel real good."

When they arrived at the apartment building, the first thing they noticed was the variety of music being played. One had B. B. King's *The Thrill is Gone* going. The second played their music lower than all the rest. It was Glenn Campbell's haunting, *Wichita Lineman*. The third played Carlos Santana's ethereal guitar licks from *Black Magic Woman*. The fourth, their destination, had a freaky guitar groove playing – The Undisputed Truths' infectious *Smiling Faces.*

"Rose, it's just time that I got my house in order and take care of business the way I should. That's the only real way I'm going to have peace. A person will never escape the demon of their past if they continue to live in denial." She didn't speak, but merely nodded. That spoke the volumes of emotions that lay within her heart. She wrinkled her nose.

The moisture in the grass from the cool of the evening stained their shoes. Once they arrived at the door, Rose rang the doorbell twice.

"Who is it?"

"It's Rose."

"All right, what's happenin'?"

"Not much, just wanted to stop by and visit for a minute, if that's alright?"

"Yeah." Vivian opened the door with a look of shock. She had on a T-shirt with a "Black Power" sign on it, blue jean cut-offs that left nothing to the imagination, and toenails painted a rich burgundy.

"So what's goin' on? What's the deal?" she said.

"I wanted to stop by and talk to you. I just asked Rose to come along with me for directions and a possible witness.

"Oh you real funny, Mr. Rufus. What you think you going to need a witness for?"

"You never know," he said, as he pursed his upper lip.

"Y'all have a seat." As they took seats on the burgundy velour sofa, they could not help but notice that the air was heavily saturated with the smell of coconut-scented incense. Vivian used them to mask the scent of her daily dose of marijuana.

"Where's the baby?" Rose asked.

"He's upstairs sleepin'. I'm just trying to chill out while he's sleep and my husband's over his cousin's house playin' cards," she said.

"So what really brings y'all this way? Did you come to see the baby, because I really don't have nothing to talk to you about, Rufus."

"I would like to see the baby, but if he's asleep, I'll do it some other time. I really wish you would let me talk to you about what's on my mind."

"What for, Rufus? I ain't in no mood for no bull. I really don't want to hear it," Vivian said. Her words came with quickness and conviction. She tapped her foot to the music as she went into the kitchen area to light her Salem Menthol cigarette on the stove's pilot light.

"Y'all got a nice piece here, Vivian. You did a good job fixin' it up," Rose said with a nervous, yet cautious smile.

"Thanks," Vivian said, her arrogance well-intact.

"So how's the baby doin'?" Rufus asked.

"He's fine."

"That's good," he said.

"So, would y'all like something to drink?" It took all that Vivian possessed to act cordial.

"I'll have a Tab," Rose said.

"I'll take a Coke," Rufus said, as his eyes wandered.

"I'll be right back with your drinks."

"Thanks."

Vivian handed them both their drinks and slumped onto the loveseat. "So, what's up? What's really goin' on?" she asked.

"The reason I stopped over was to see how you were doin'," Rufus said, holding his hands in a praying position, in order to emphasize every word.

"Fine, and what else?"

"Just let me finish, Vivian. What I've really got to say is not the easiest thing for me to do."

"You never had a problem up 'til now. So why can't you speak your mind?"

"All right." Rufus took in a deep breath. His eyes careened upward, as if in search of reason.

"Vivian, if there're any negative feelings you have toward me or any bad blood, I want to make it right tonight. I want it out in the open so that we can deal with it and try and resolve it. Whatever it takes, I just want you to know that I want to do the right thing by you."

"Well ain't that something. Your conscience must be really working on you," she said.

"Maybe so," he said, as he squirmed around in uncomfortable fashion on the sofa. Vivian, on the other hand, seemed relaxed.

"Well, what do you think, Rufus? Do you think I should be mad, upset or what?" "

"Probably so."

"Man, you better get a grip. You know good and well things ain't right without me havin' to even say anything about it."

"Yes, Vivian, I know and all I can do is ask you for your forgiveness."

"I'm not one for holdin' grudges. I just want you to do right by your son, that's all," Vivian said, gesturing with her hands.

"And I have every intention on doing just that." Vivian's silence suspended all the inertia in the room.

"I don't know what else to tell you, Rufus. My life is goin' on. I got some happiness. I got my son. I just want you to do your part and you know what your part is. I don't have to tell you."

"I'm going to do the right thing, Vivian, and that's why I'm here asking for your forgiveness and to let you know that I'm here for the baby."

"I'm just trippin' that you had the nerve to even come over here. Don't get me wrong. I respect what you're sayin'. I can forgive you, but like I said, just do the right thing, Rufus."

"I appreciate your forgiveness. I'll be there for him. He's my flesh and blood. After I go off the scene, people will be sayin' about him 'Man, that's Rufus Johnson's boy.' That's why I want him to know that I am his father."

"That sounds good and that makes a lot of sense, but why now, Rufus? What have you done for him since he's been born? Nothin'. That's my concern," Vivian said.

"I was wrong. I know that. But I want to put that behind me now."

Her voice shifted into the defensive. "I ain't tryin' to hear your lies and excuses as to why you didn't. I just want you to do so from now on."

"That's what I intend on doin'," he said, with a plea for understanding.

"You gotta know, Rufus, that the way you handled this whole thing was wrong. You ignored me. That hurt. I had to go through the pain and embarrassment of it on my own. I needed you to be there and you weren't," she said, while moving her head to the rhythm of her words. Beads of perspiration were forming on her forehead.

"You got me on that, Vivian."

"I know I got you."

"There ain't nothing I can do about goin' back into history and changing anything. I can't, you know that. All I can do is try and be the best man that I can be from here on out. Not perfect, just a better man. That's what God requires, that we give our best."

"Can you do that?" she asked.

"Yes."

The Rose from Sharon

"I'll have to see, Rufus. That's all I can say," she said, shaking her head, feeling worn already.

"Just the fact that I came over here should be enough evidence to show you that I'm serious." Vivian was not fully convinced that he came over with the right motive. She felt it was to stop his conscience from eating him up.

"You said earlier that you forgave me. Right now it's kind of hard to tell."

"Don't go getting smart, Rufus," she said. Her voice, now in a tone of youthful jazziness, was like an alto sax.

"I'm not, I'm just telling you how you're makin' me feel."

"Oh, I'm sorry." Vivian said in a voice of deliberate sarcasm. Before she could say another word, the doorbell rang. Della and Larry were standing in the doorway looking angry and tense. "What is it y'all want?" Vivian asked.

"You gotta lot of nerve talking to me like that. I just want to know if Rose Johnson is here."

"Yeah, she's here, but don't be getting jazzy with me, cause I ain't putting up with it!" Vivian said.

"Ain't nobody getting jazzy with you. I think you need to learn some respect though. I know your mother didn't raise you to talk to grown folk the way you do."

"Whatever. Yeah, Rose is here with her daddy."

"Yeah, I know. I see his car out front. May I come in and speak to her?"

"I guess. What are y'all tryin to do, have a family reunion in my crib?" Vivian asked.

They walked by, as Vivian held open the door.

"What's up, Larry."

"Not much. What's happnin', Viv?" A noxious anger burned in Della's eyes like the flames that kiss the cool autumn sky during an October bonfire. She did all she could to stay composed, but she couldn't stop staring at Vivian.

Out of the blue, Della hollered at Vivian, "Bitch, I oughta kill you!!" She went out of character and took off after Vivian. Rufus grabbed her tightly before she reached her.

"I oughta just kill you!" Della yelled again.

"Let her go. Here I am, if you want to kill me," Vivian hollered out.

"You can go straight to hell, Rufus. This is all your fault. This wouldn't never of happened if you wouldn't have started up with her!" Della hollered. While trying to twist out of his grip, the strap of her bra snapped.

"Della, you really need to try to calm down. This don't make no sense," he said.

"You gotta lotta nerve talking bout that don't make sense. You messin' around on me! That's what don't make sense. All I came over here to do was to get Rose. I don't need all of this, Rufus. I just don't need it!" she hollered.

Rose's eyes began to well up. She felt betrayed as she watched these two towers of strength and love now locked in a cold matrix of civil war.

"I know I've been wrong. I just came over here to try and straighten out some of the wrong that I've done. I definitely didn't come over here for any trouble." Della unleashed her most vile strength and landed a slap on his face that stunned his sense of reality. It felt like a punch. He slowly, carefully rubbed his cheek and backed up two steps. A cascade of stars played for the better part of six minutes. It event took Vivian by surprise.

"I think it would be a good idea if all y'all just left before someone gets hurt for real."

"Yeah, I think you're right," Rufus said. They all slowly began to depart through the door with the equal regret of loved ones who leave the cemetery after a funeral. Della continued to roll her eyes at Vivian. The cool air struck their faces with the force of a wind that rages through a tunnel. Rufus swallowed hard. His throat was dry.

"Della why don't you let me stop by the house? I got some things I want to discuss with you," he said. The timbre of his voice was calm and subtle.

"Like what? Don't you think we discussed enough tonight? I mean, ain't you had enough of me for one night, Rufus?"

"I ain't comin' over to fight or argue. I just want to talk over some things with you, that's all."

"Some things like what? I ain't really tryin' to hear anything

The Rose from Sharon

that you sayin', man."

"I've got one more stone left in my shoe that's naggin' at me and you're the only one who can remove it."

"You need to take your shoe off and remove it yourself. I think that's what you'd be better off doin'," Della said.

"I mean something's naggin' at me. Listen, if you would just let me say what I feel I need to say then you can do whatever it is you need to do. I won't bother you no more," he said, while wringing his hands.

"So why can't you talk to me right now, if it's all that important?"

"This just ain't the time or the place."

"You can't stay, Rufus. I've got to be up early," she said. Rufus shook his head, as if in agreement.

"I understand. I won't be long." He turned on the car and adjusted the heat before he
followed behind them.

When they arrived at the house, Della sat on the sofa. Rufus chose the smallest chair in the room. "So what's on your mind, Rufus?" she said with the same ferocity that a prizefighter uses in cornering their most formidable opponent.

"There's been a lot of things on my mind. But right now, the main thing is your feelings."

"Feelings about what, Rufus? Come on now. I ain't in no mood for your silliness tonight. I'm really not," she said in an aggravated tone.

"I'm not playin', Della. I want to know what you feel about everything that has happened."

"You gotta ask!? You should already know how upset I am about all of this."

"I do know, Della. I'm so embarrassed, I don't really even know what to say."

"What made you want to go around messin' with young girls like that? Are you nuts or what?"

"I don't know, Della. I don't know. I can't erase the past. I just have to learn from it. The thing that I'm tryin' to get to, Della, is that tonight is all that matters right now."

"Right now, huh, Rufus?"

"Tonight. This moment. Right now is all that we have. Tomorrow morning isn't promised to either one of us."

"I know that," she said.

"Tell me this, Della. Would you feel bad if I were to die tonight without me ever telling you what's on my mind?" Della looked helpless and hesitant in her response.

"I would feel bed. I wouldn't even wish death on you right now. Besides, that might be too easy for you. You need to live a little longer so you can suffer some more."

"If that's how you feel, I respect your feelings," he said.

"Now what's on your mind, Rufus?"

"I just wanted to tell you that I'm sorry for all the wrong that I've done and for any hurt that I've caused you. I'm really sorry."

"Now your sorry?" she said.

"I've felt bad about this for a long time Della. I've told you that before."

"I really don't even know what to say to you, Rufus. You lied, you cheated, and now I'm s'pose to just open my heart and forgive you? Just like that?"

"I know it's askin' a lot to forgive me and if you didn't, I would understand why, even though it would hurt me. It's just that my life feels incomplete knowing that we couldn't get over this. We've been through a lot together, Della."

"Yeah, but nothing like this," she said, her mind reliving the anger, rage and humiliation.

"I've cried many a night over this, Della."

"So have I," she said, as she slowly raised herself from the sofa. "Listen, Rufus. I really don't know what else to say to you. I'm through with all this."

"Through with what?" he asked with intensity.

"I'm through with us. What did you think I meant? There's nothing left to give, Rufus. The trust is gone. The love is gone. What's left?" All of his fortitude was used to blink back tears that threatened to spill over.

The Rose from Sharon

"I do still love you, Della," he said, his eyes focused directly upon her.

"Come on now. You ain't even bein' real if you believe that, because if you loved me you wouldn't..."

He quickly cut her off. "What? I made a mistake. Everybody makes mistakes. Even you." Rufus was now standing up face to face with her.

"I wouldn't have done that to you," she said.

"You're a better person than me then. You may not have done that, but there are probably other things you would have done. Sin is sin, no matter what it is. Wrong is wrong, no matter who does it."

"Yeah, that might be true, but why can't you accept that we can't stay together any longer?" Rufus began to bite his lower lip. The weight of her words weakened him. He was unable to respond. His heart fluttered.

"It's not that I can't accept it. I just don't want to accept it."

"There's nothin' you can do to make it up to me." Determination expelled itself from her voice.

"Nothin?" he asked.

"Nothin!" Concern came from Della as she noticed the beads of sweat that formed on Rufus's forehead. "Are you alright?" she asked.

He didn't give an answer. He simply stared at a corner of the room. She asked again, "Rufus, are you alright?" He held his peace and while in the process of doing so, his mind took a chronological trip down the journey of their marriage.

"Why would you say that it was over?"

"It's the best thing for both of us," Della said, as he continued to reel within the measure of his mind. He prayed like all was on the line, with God's Will being the theme that pulled him through to the other end.

He began to speak, as if given authority from on high. "Della, all of us miss the mark sometimes. The difference is in the ones who are sorry for what they did and the ones who really don't care about the ones they've hurt. God can change a person's heart, if they let Him, Della."

"I know that." The words 'Forgive and ye shall be forgiven' took over Della's mind. It penetrated her spirit. Then came the words, 'You cannot remove the splinter from your neighbor's eyes when you have a beam in your own eye.' Scripture after scripture burned within her: 'All have sinned and fallen short of the glory of God.'

She tried denying its effect.

Right before her eyes, the one that sent her was 'Judge and ye shall not be judged, for what measure you mete, it shall be measured back to you.' She fought back the tears. She looked upward as if in counsel with God. Her fists were clinched tightly. Within minutes, she was smiling, but wasn't quite sure why.

"This is really crazy. Sometimes, I think I have all the answers to all of the problems, but I don't. I really don't," she said.

"Nobody does. That's why we have to look to the One who does," Rufus said. He smiled, then slightly raised his head.

"You're right, Rufus. As God is my witness, my mind had been made up about you. But, I ain't never had God deal with me the way He just has. I'm sorry for judging you and I do forgive you and you need to start bringin' your stuff back home where it belongs."

'Della, I love you," he said, as they embraced.

"Rufus, all I can say is that God's Will is stronger than my will and He always has the last say."

"You don't have to say anymore. That says it all."

A smile came over Rose's face as she listened to every word while sitting quietly on the top step of the stairs.

God had answered her prayer, as she said silently, "Thank you."

About the Author

Stuart Abrams has been writing professionally for the past 10 years. He resides in Sandusky, Ohio and holds a bachelors degree in business administration. He currently is pursuing a Masters of Business Administration degree from Tiffin University. "The Rose from Sharon" is Abrams second novel, and his first, the seminal "More than Conquerors" was lauded as being "intensely written". The local Sandusky Library listed Abrams with such writers as Toni Morrison, James Baldwin and Ralph Ellison. Abrams is currently working on his next novel "He who is without sin". A story set in the late 80's about a prominent Midwest pastor who is wrongfully accused of extorting money from his church.

Printed in the United States
43024LVS00006B/100-117